2010

The D:
Wore Dia

D0947358

by Mark Schweizer

Liturgical Mysteries
by Mark Schweizer

Why do people keep dying in the little town of St. Germaine, North Carolina? It's hard to say. Maybe there's something in the water. Whatever the reason, it certainly has *nothing* to do with St. Barnabas Episcopal Church!

*Murder in the choirloft. A choir-director detective.
They're not what you expect...they're even funnier!*

The Alto Wore Tweed
The Baritone Wore Chiffon
The Tenor Wore Tapshoes
The Soprano Wore Falsettos
The Bass Wore Scales
The Mezzo Wore Mink
The Diva Wore Diamonds

**ALL SEVEN now available at
your favorite mystery bookseller or sjmpbooks.com.**

"It's like Mitford meets Jurassic Park, only without the wisteria and the dinosaurs..."

Advance Praise for *The Diva Wore Diamonds*

"This book is the onion of mystery novels. Each layer, peeled back, reveals another, and every one of them makes you cry."
Nancy Jones, CPA

"I used to be a nobody, but now I have a quote in a book!"
John Perdue, student and incidental character

"*The Diva Wore Diamonds*—the culmination of Intelligent Design."
Chuck Darwin, part-time plumber

"I haven't been able to stop thinking about this beautiful book. I laughed, I cried, it became a part of me..."
Mitsy Garnet, professional on-line book reviewer ($9.95 per review)

"It's very difficult to make any comment on a piece of writing which, in a very real sense, is beyond criticism..."
Richard Shephard, Chamberlain, York Minster

"Yeah, it's full of mistakes, but it just makes you go, hey! this guy doesn't care what the fat-cat literazzi think! That's just how he rolls, Dog!"
Dwayne Lee Putnam, book reviewer, Mobile Home Quarterly

"This book is the *Pachelbel Canon* of words."
Nada Fuqua, soprano

"Sparkly!"
Bambi Timberlake, St. James Music Press unpaid summer intern

"As smooth as three-day-old Scotch."
Dr. Ken Dougherty, M.D.

"An integral part of the nation's economic stimulus program. Buy this book immediately!"
Name Withheld, Secretary of the Treasury

"The Heimlich Maneuver of novels."
Karen Shields, elementary school principal

"I am not responsible for my husband's debts."
Donis Schweizer, wife

For the Divas

The Diva Wore Diamonds
A Liturgical Mystery
Copyright ©2009 by Mark Schweizer

Illustrations by Jim Hunt
www.jimhuntillustration.com

Published by
St. James Music Press
www.sjmpbooks.com
P.O. Box 1009
Hopkinsville, KY 42241-1009

ISBN 978-0-9721211-5-6

1st Printing May, 2009

Acknowledgements
Holly Derickson, Sandy Cavanah, Nancy Cooper, Beverly Easterling,
Marty Hatteberg, Kristen Linduff, Patricia Nakamura, Donis Schweizer,
Liz Schweizer, Richard Shephard, John Schrecker,
and Robert Wyke

Prelude

"Did you know Raymond Chandler wrote poetry?" Meg asked. She was sitting on the sofa, a biography of Chandler in one hand, a grilled cheese sandwich in the other, devouring them both in turn.

"I didn't know that."

"Maybe you should try penning a verse or two."

"Hmm," I said. "That'd look good on the resumé. Detective Hayden Konig, police chief and purveyor of iambic pentameter."

I pushed back from the writing desk and nudged the hat back on my head. Once Raymond Chandler's hat, but mine now. Chandler memorabilia shows up in auctions now and then. Mostly letters. Some signed pictures. Occasionally a screenplay or a manuscript. The hat was a coup. That it fit me was courtesy of my haberdasher. That I could afford it was thanks to a lot of luck and good timing. In addition to the fedora, I also owned Raymond Chandler's typewriter, an Underwood No. 5. That it still worked was a testament to the most successful typewriter design in history. That it would work for me as well as it worked for the old wordsmith was still in question, at least as far as Meg was concerned.

"I suggest a love poem," said Meg. "It says here that Chandler was a romantic."

"Yep," I said. "Author of the immortal line, 'She smelled the way the Taj Mahal looks by moonlight.'"

"He wrote that? Eeew."

"Well, he was obviously in love. Besides," I said, "I've written a lot of poems. Love poems."

"Oh, puhlease!" Meg rolled her eyes and gave Baxter the crust of her sandwich, a morsel he'd been eyeing for the better part of ten minutes. Being a dog of infinite patience and nobility, he was grateful as only a canine can be, and his tail thumped heavily against the side of the sofa. Meg scratched him behind the ears and looked over at me.

"You cannot count 'Oh, Eileen, you're so keen, won't you be my beauty queen?' as a love poem."

"It's a perfectly good love poem," I countered. "Eileen being your middle name. I couldn't rhyme anything with 'Megan' except 'vegan' or 'pagan,' and you're not either one."

"How about 'Ronald Reagan?'" said Meg with a giggle.

"Don't talk to me now," I said, with a dismissive wave of my hand. "I'm getting inspired."

The typewriter stared up at me from the amber glow that the green-shaded bank light cast across the desk, its alphabet teeth grinning, anxious to resume their insistent chatter. I rolled my shoulders, shaking out some imagined stiffness, and typed out some Chandlerisms to warm up. I always found that a few well-turned phrases served to awaken the muse.

Dead men are heavier than broken hearts.

I loved the way the words looked on the page and loved knowing that I'd typed the very same sentence on the very same typewriter that Raymond Chandler had used in 1939. My fingers tingled. I put a cigar in my mouth and chomped down on it. I didn't light it. Now that I was married, I only lit up outdoors or maybe when Meg was gone for a few days.

At three A.M. I was walking the floor, listening to Khachaturyan working in a tractor factory. He called it a violin concerto. I called it a loose fan belt and the hell with it.

"How's it going?" asked Meg.

"Still warming up," I said. "I'm not quite ready."

"Warm-ups? So, you're sort of like a virtuoso," Meg said. "The Yo-Yo Ma of bad writing."

"Exactly." I laced my fingers together, turned my palms out, stretched my arms, and cracked my knuckles in the time-honored fashion of writers everywhere.

"How about some toe-touches?"

"Already did them," I lied.

"The choir will be happy to get a new story," said Meg, "as awful as it may be. It's been over a year since the last one." Meg could hold a conversation and read at the same time, something I couldn't fathom. She flipped a page. "Here's something, Hayden. Did you know that Raymond Chandler had a much older wife?"

"I did know that. Her name was Cissy. She told him to quit writing out of the side of his mouth."

"He didn't take her advice," Meg said. "Good thing."

"I shall not bother to point out the obvious similarities between Cissy's unfair criticism and another wife who shall remain beautiful but nameless."

"Not the same thing at all," said Meg. "Chandler was a good writer. You're a bad writer." She smiled sweetly. "See the difference?"

"Yes," I said. "But, bad or not, my public has been denied for too long. The time has come."

"The muse has struck?"

"Like Big Ben on steroids." I pulled the used paper out of the typewriter and inserted a piece of 24 lb. bond behind the roller. Then with a few clicks of the return bar, I was ready. My fingers drifted slowly down to the glass keys.

The Diva Wore Diamonds
Chapter One

Brilliant.

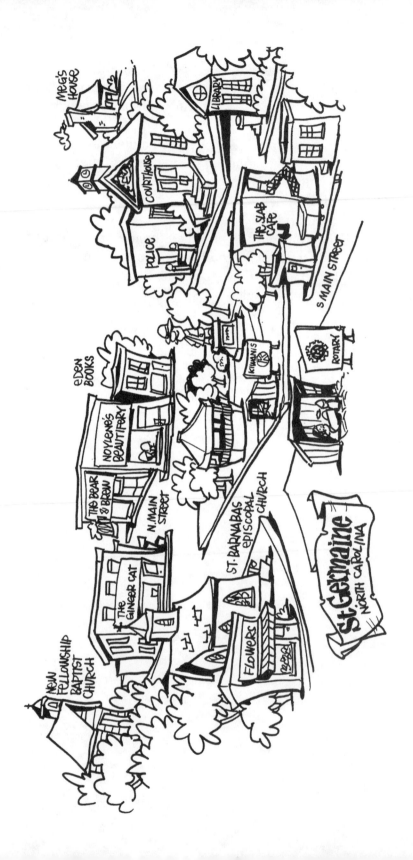

Chapter One

A church fire is a terrible thing. The night that St. Barnabas burned to the ground, most of the parishioners were there attending a Thanksgiving pageant. Once the fire had been discovered, it didn't take long for everyone inside to exit and gather in the park across the street. There were those who wept, those who cursed, and those who watched silently as the old, familiar structure lit the clear November sky, then finally collapsed on itself in a holocaust of sparks, flames, and snapping timbers. The volunteer fire department had done its best, but was chiefly concerned with keeping the inferno from consuming the rest of the downtown square. The firemen did a heroic job, working far into the night, and the newly-elected mayor of St. Germaine, Cynthia Johnsson, gave them all commendations at the next town meeting.

Mercifully, the church was all that burned. Not a soul was hurt—no one we could find, anyway. Collette, Dave Vance's ex-fiancée, had disappeared, but we had to assume that she went back to Spartanburg. Nobody looked too hard.

In the nineteen months that followed the fire, a lot had happened in our little village. This is the way of all small towns, and St. Germaine, North Carolina, is no exception. Babies are born, people marry, old folks die, children grow up, businesses open and close, families come and go, and everyone knows everyone else's business. The grapevine in a small town is something that cannot be overestimated, and the grapevine was in full flower on this summer morning.

"Hayden, did you hear about Bud?" asked Noylene, filling my coffee cup for the third time in as many passes, at the same time balancing two plates of pancakes and a Pete's Breakfast Special up her free arm.

"Enlighten me," I said, picking up one of the made-from-scratch biscuits, splitting it with my butter knife, and layering it with homemade cherry preserves.

"He's got a scholarship to Harvard!"

Pete, inventor of Pete's Breakfast Special and the owner of the Slab Café, rolled his eyes.

I took a bite of the biscuit and chased it down with a sip of coffee. "Harvard? You don't say. Good for him."

"Wait till I tell Wormy." Noylene scuttled off to deliver the rest of her orders.

"An hour ago, it was Georgetown," said Pete. "Before that, UNC Chapel Hill. What's the real story?"

"Davidson College," I said. "No scholarship, but he got in. He's heading out in the fall."

"Good for him," said Pete. "Did he get a good financial aid package?"

"Yep."

Bud was the eldest of the McCollough children, all of them named for the thing that their father, PeeDee, loved more than life itself: beer. After Bud came Pauli Girl, now almost seventeen and as beautiful as her mother, Ardine, must have been in her youth, before life in the hills wore her down. Last in line to the McCollough fortune, a fortune consisting of a single-wide trailer and PeeDee's old pick-up truck, was ten-year-old Moose-Head, Moosey for short. He was easily identifiable to everyone in town by his mop of hair, his old-fashioned pair of high-top Keds, and the fact that he was always moving at the speed of a hummingbird. He'd gotten a pair of glasses last fall, after Ardine finally managed to get him in to see the optometrist.

Ardine had raised the three kids by herself ever since PeeDee had disappeared some ten years ago. PeeDee was an abusive husband and father, and everyone agreed to pretend that he'd run off with some floozy he'd met at the truck stop down on State Road 321. In fact, he was now probably food for worms somewhere up in Bucksnort Holler. Ardine was not a woman to mess with, and the whispers were that, after Moosey was born, she'd had just about all she wanted of PeeDee McCollough.

"What's ol' Bud going to major in?" asked Pete.

I shrugged. "He's got a couple years of a liberal arts curriculum to do first. Then he's thinking about an interdisciplinary major. That'll probably change. Most kids don't end up where they start."

"That's for sure," said Pete. "I started in pre-med. Now, here I am, the owner of this fine eating establishment."

He gestured around the Slab Café. The corner diner on the town square featured a long countertop adorned with sugar shakers, ketchup bottles, salt and pepper shakers and a couple of covered cake plates. Six swivel-stools were bolted into the floor in front of the counter. Eighteen-inch black and white squares of linoleum covered the floor in a checkerboard pattern from the front door to the kitchen. In the center of the restaurant were several tables covered with tablecloths and flanked by wooden chairs. Four booths on the far wall completed the customer seating. The fabric of choice, seat cushions to tablecloths, menu covers to place-mats, was Naugahyde. Red Naugahyde. Decor courtesy of Noylene Fabergé-Dupont, the early-morning waitress and owner of "Noylene's Beautifery, an oasis of allurement, Dip-N-Tan by appointment only."

I laughed. "I remember that you didn't last a semester in pre-med."

Pete shrugged and took a sip of his coffee. "I could have done it," he said. "Brain surgery is nothing compared to running a profitable diner."

Pete Moss and I go way back. He was my roommate in college, and I was best man at his first three weddings. We'd both graduated with music degrees; then Pete headed for the Army Band while I added a master's degree and another in Criminal Justice to my resumé. After his stint in the military, Pete came home to St. Germaine, opened his café and rose to the respectable office of mayor. It was from this exalted position that he called me and offered me the post of police chief, a job I still have, even though Pete has since been deposed and relegated to the lowly status of just another tax-paying citizen with a grudge against the government.

The cowbell hanging on the door of the Slab jangled. Nancy Parsky came in, followed closely by Dave Vance—the other two dedicated crime fighters on the St. Germaine police force. Nancy was wearing her uniform, a contrast to my standard faded jeans and polo shirt. Dave was in his khakis and button-down blue oxford, sleeves rolled up in deference to the summer season. They wasted no time in pulling up a couple of chairs and diggng into the biscuits and gravy.

"Good morning to you, too," said Pete.

"Mmph," said Dave.

"I second that," said Nancy, swallowing her bite in a hasty gulp. "I agree with Dave. Mmph."

The bell clanked again, and Cynthia Johnsson rushed in, tying her apron behind her as she headed for the kitchen. "Sorry, sorry, sorry..." she said, disappearing behind the swinging door.

Pete shook his head. "I tell you, you just can't get good help anymore."

Cynthia reappeared with a coffee pot in her hand. "Sorry, sorry," she muttered, filling the cup in front of Nancy. She offered a thin smile to Pete, gave his gray ponytail a playful tug, and kissed him on the top of his balding head. "Sorry, honey. I just don't know where the time went." She poured Dave a cup and topped mine off before heading to a table of out-of-town patrons who were glaring angrily at the menu and looking pointedly around for someone to take their order. People from south Florida who visit St. Germaine in the summer for our climate do not take kindly to being made to wait for their breakfast. They are used to being in a hurry and having many important things to do. That they normally don't mind waiting in traffic for two hours on any given day to drive to and from work is immaterial. That there really isn't anything to do in St. Germaine before nine a.m. hasn't occurred to them yet.

"Did Noylene leave already?" asked Dave.

"I expect she's out back taking her break," said Pete. "She's not off until ten, but she needs at least three smokes per shift, and nothing's going to stop her."

Cynthia Johnsson, our tardy waitress, is also the current mayor of St. Germaine and Pete Moss' significant other. Being mayor doesn't pay very much—certainly not enough to live on—and Cynthia is a first-rate waitress, having served at all the fine eating establishments in town at one time or another. During the summer months, she holds down the eight to twelve shift at the Slab, the twelve to three shift at The Ginger Cat across the square, and the five to closing shift at the Bear and Brew. Every day except Mondays. She's off on Mondays. Cynthia's also a professional belly-dancer, available for parties and individual instruction.

"As soon as Noylene comes back in, we can have our meeting," I noted. "We really should wait for the mayor to finish pouring coffee."

Pete snorted.

"I hear y'all are back in the church this Sunday," said Nancy.

"Nope. A week from Sunday," I said. "It's been a long nineteen months."

"St. B looks the same as it did before the fire," said Dave. "Any fancy improvements?"

12

"Like what?" I asked.

"You know...big screens that lower from the ceiling. Maybe a hydraulic platform for the praise band."

"You're an idiot," said Nancy. "Pass me another biscuit."

"There are security cameras now," I said. "A whole security system, in fact. And we have some solar panels on the roof. Very green. Very environmentally conscious."

"The insurance pay for that?" asked Pete.

"Nope. But the building committee felt we could afford the upgrade. The solar panels won't provide enough electricity to run the church, but they'll help."

"I affirm their greenyness," said Cynthia as she passed by the table, still pursuing her quest to make sure everyone's coffee cups were full. "As mayor, it's my solemn duty—"

"Miss! Hey! Miss!" called one of the excessively tanned Floridians from across the restaurant. He rattled his cup rudely on the table top. Cynthia gritted her teeth and headed his direction.

"There are other things, of course," I continued. "The offices have been rearranged. Bathrooms moved. Stuff like that. But, all in all, the church looks very much like the old St. Barnabas."

"How about the organ?" asked Nancy. "Have they finished it yet?"

"Not yet. There's still about a week of installation to do, then the final voicing. It should be ready for the first Sunday we're back. If not all of it, enough to make a noble noise."

I'm privy to this inside knowledge because, in addition to being the police chief of St. Germaine, I'm also employed as the organist and choir director at St. Barnabas Episcopal Church. It isn't a job I need. It's a job I like. In fact, I like both my jobs, demonstrated by the fact that I'm still doing them. If I didn't enjoy working, I'd be sitting in my fancy log cabin on my two-hundred acres, counting my money, a task that would take a long time because I have a lot of it thanks to a little invention I patented about fifteen years ago and a very wise and sexy investment counselor. So sexy, in fact, that I married her. Meg is the best in the biz and even after the downturn in the market, I was still sitting pretty.

"I can't wait to hear it," said Nancy. "The King of Instruments."

"It's a beaut!" I said. "Almost a year and a half in the making."

I had called the Baum-Boltoph Organ Company within a few

days of the fire. They'd done the rebuilding of the organ ten years ago, and I'd made some fast friends, including Michael Baum, the owner. After the new organ committee visited five of the instruments the company had designed and built and had seen Michael's presentation, Baum-Boltoph was the unanimous choice to build our new organ. It took a bit of doing to move up on their list, but what are friends for? Now, almost a year and a half later, the organ had been completed, and the installation was well underway. Since the fire, the church had been meeting in the rotunda of the courthouse, and I'd been playing a grand piano that the church bought and moved in for the services. The piano would end up in the parish hall, and I was ready to get back behind the console of an instrument that the congregation could complain about. "Could the priest please do something about the organ? It's too loud." Loud? They hadn't *heard* loud. Not yet.

I looked out the plate glass window of the Slab and across Sterling Park to where the new St. Barnabas Church stood. The mason's helpers were meandering to and fro, cleaning up the remnants of the stonework. Old scaffolds were being unbolted and stacked in beat-up construction trucks. A painter was working on the front door, applying the second or maybe third coat of dark red paint—red: the traditional color of church doors offering sanctuary to any offender. There were some landscapers in front as well, putting in the sprinkler system and making a general mess of the lawn. Most of what was left to be done, though, was the finish work on the inside. The pews were due to arrive from New England in the next couple of days, the light fixtures for the nave were on a truck somewhere between St. Louis and Asheville, and the sound system wasn't working. The contractor would be scrambling to get everything finished in two weeks.

Cynthia, seeing Noylene come through the swinging kitchen door, plopped down at our table with a huff.

"I swear..." she grumbled. "I'm starting to hate tourists."

"You're the mayor," said Pete with an evil grin. "You must embrace the tourist trade. Take them to your bosom, as it were."

"My bosom is not up for company," said Cynthia.

"All bosoms aside," I said, "now that we're all here, what's on the agenda for the week?"

Pete took a sip of his coffee and raised his eyebrows. Nancy shrugged. Dave helped himself to another biscuit.

"Well, that's it, then." I started to get up.

"Hang on," said Cynthia. "We have the referendum coming up on Sunday beer and wine sales. The Bear and Brew wants to sell beer on Sunday afternoon and evening during the football games. Right now, there's a city ordinance against it. You can buy beer at the Piggly Wiggly, but you can't buy it in a restaurant. How silly is that?"

I sat back down.

"I agree," said Pete. "But there's no sense worrying about it now. It's on the ballot."

"When's the vote?" asked Nancy.

"A week from tomorrow," said Cynthia. "Shouldn't I be making speeches or something?"

"Anything else need voting on?" I asked.

"Annexation of about five hundred acres to include the Blueridge Furs and Camp Possumtickle. They both asked. They'd like fire and police protection and don't mind paying the extra taxes. The City Council was all for it, but it has to be voted on."

"You mean Camp Daystar," said Dave. "It's still a Christian nudist camp."

"Not a very exciting election," said Nancy. "I'll bet we don't have three hundred people vote on Tuesday."

"Have you advertised the liquor referendum?" I asked.

"The listings come out in the paper tomorrow morning. One week before the election. That's what our city charter says."

"So," said Pete with a grin, "no one knows about it yet."

"Well, obviously the council knows. Maybe others. I don't know for sure, but it's not a secret."

"I expect you'll be pretty busy starting tomorrow," I said. "Nothing like liquor and nudists to get folks riled up."

"Oh, man," said Cynthia. "I'm doomed. Any good news? How about the parking ticket problem?"

"Taken care of," said Nancy. "Here's our plan. We'll continue to give out tickets, and people will continue to throw them down in the street. Then, after a while, we'll send them a bill, and they'll ignore it. After a few months, we'll delete it from their record."

"It's called the 'circle of life,'" said Dave.

"But what about the revenue?" asked Cynthia.

"We really don't need it," I said. "Property taxes are so high that we run a surplus every year anyway. It's not like we're in a budget crisis. The City Council has a couple of million dollars in the coffers."

"It's the principle of the thing!"

"I have a suggestion," said Pete. "Why not declare an unofficial moratorium on parking tickets and let these tourists park where they want during the summer? They're here to spend money. No sense in making them mad."

"Fine with me," said Nancy. Dave nodded.

"Don't I need to bring this to the City Council?"

"You certainly can if you want," said Pete. "But by the time they've finished discussing it, talking to their constituents, floating a few trial balloons, and deciding how to vote to make the least number of people mad, it'll be March of next year before they do anything. Even then, they'll probably decide we need to give *more* parking tickets. I've said it before, and I'll say it again—democracy just doesn't work."

Cynthia looked confused. "So...you're saying..."

"It's easy," I said. "We'll just quit giving tickets to cars with out-of-county tags. No law against *not* giving out parking tickets." I gave her a palms-up shrug. "We don't advertise it. We just don't do it."

"I'm beginning to understand," said Cynthia. "The system really *doesn't* work."

"Never has, never will," said Pete.

"Miss!" barked the obnoxious Floridian. "Hey you! The waitress sitting down!"

Cynthia stood with a sigh. "Could you give those bozos one last parking ticket just for my sake?"

"Tell you what, Madam Mayor," said Nancy, with an evil grin. "I'll light 'em up on their way out of town. They'll be speeding. I can tell just by looking at them."

Chapter 2

The smell of grilling hamburgers greeted me as I came in the kitchen door. Hamburgers and onions, Swiss cheese, potato chips, cole slaw, and a cold bottle of Ringwood Old Thumper Extra Special Ale. Of course, this all might be just a case of wishful smelling. I was sure about the hamburger, though, and I knew I had a few bottles of Old Thumper left in the fridge.

I walked up behind Meg and put my arms around her waist.

"Glad you could make it," she said without turning. Her black hair was pulled up high on her head, and I buried a kiss on the back of her neck.

"I wouldn't miss 'Hamburger Night.'"

"This isn't 'Hamburger Night.' We don't have 'Hamburger Night.' I just happen to be fixing hamburgers."

"At night."

"Yes," she laughed. "At night. But it's not... oh, never mind."

"I just love 'Hamburger Night,'" I said, opening the refrigerator door and rooting around until I came up with Mr. Thumper. Before Meg and I got married, my fridge contained beer, knockwurst, sauerkraut and some dead mice. The dead mice were for Archimedes, the barn owl who came and went as he pleased, and was an endless fascination to both of us. Archimedes used a window above the kitchen sink equipped with an electric-eye, and it wasn't unusual to wake up in the morning, walk into the living room, and see him perched on the head of the stuffed buffalo. Now my refrigerator contained humus, low-fat yogurt, some kind of salad that tasted like nettles, fava beans, free range quail eggs, and who knew what else. Luckily there was still room for a couple of brews. I kept the mice in the spare fridge in the garage.

"Save one of those beers for dinner," said Meg. "It'll be ready in fifteen minutes."

"Just enough time to finish my chapter."

I took my beer out of the kitchen and into the den. I'd had this house built when I moved to St. Germaine, and it was designed around an old log cabin that I bought, dismantled and moved from Kentucky. The original cabin, a twenty by twenty, two-story structure crafted in 1842, comprised the den, but the rest of the house was mountain chic. Meg had a house in town. That is, *we* had a house in town, as well as the one up here in the hollers. Ruby, Meg's mother, lived in that house, and Meg, like the good daughter she was, spent the occasional night in town to keep her company.

I clicked the remote to the stereo, a WAV system coupled with a 100 CD changer, and listened as the music of Edward Elgar filled the house. Then, sitting at my desk and reading the few sentences on the paper still in my typewriter, I put down the beer, stuck an unlit cigar between my teeth, put on my writing hat, and started banging on the old keys.

•••

The Diva Wore Diamonds
Chapter One

In the beginning there was God, but then there was some trouble in the Garden of Eden, and then a scooter crashed into the front of a bar, but I'm getting ahead of my story.

Praise and Worship pastor Wiggy Newland was dead-- dead as Sunday night church. He had a reputation as a ladies' man; a real looker with a mullet, more gold chains than Mr. T's pawn shop, and enough hair on his chest to make a coat for a very small Hungarian, but his pearly-gate smile belied a heart as black as the hand-stitched ostrich skin cover of his Mel Gibson Study Bible, not like its First Corinthians with its "love is patient, love is kind," but the part in Deuteronomy where God smites you with hemorrhoids.

"You know this mug?"

The voice belonged to Detective Jack Hammer, a bull that had been on the job so long that he could remember Preparation A and was as tough as a boiled owl. Me? I'm a Liturgy Detective. Duly licensed by the Diocese of North Carolina and accountable only to the Bishop. That's what it said on my card and, with the economy what it is, I was inclined to agree.

"Gimme an answer, flatfoot," Hammer said.

"Yeah, I knew him. Wiggy Newland."

"Know who would want to kill him?"

Hammer reminded me of one of the Three Stooges, either Curly or Larry--you know, the one who goes "woo woo woo." I lit up a stogie. "Sure. Everyone that met him."

Hammer snorted and frisked the body with the deftness of Sarah Palin skinning a baby moose. "So, why are you here?"

"The bishops sent me over. Gotta keep a lid on this one," I said. "Wiggy had the goods on a few of the higher-ups."

"They care who killed him?"

"Nope," I shrugged. "Probably glad he's dead. They want his files."

"Not a chance," grunted Hammer. "Evidence."

"Only if you find 'em before I do," I muttered.

•••

"Supper's ready!" came the call from the kitchen. "And leave that cigar on your desk."

I collected my beer and followed my nose into the kitchen. Meg was already sitting at the table.

"Nice music," said Meg.

"Nice burgers," I replied.

"Holst?"

I shook my head. "Close. It's Elgar." I hefted the burger. "Moose?"

"Close. It's cow." said Meg. "Where am I going to get moose in St. Germaine?"

"At the Piggly Wiggly?"

"Oh, sure," said Meg. "I forgot about the giant hooved herbivore section at the Piggly Wiggly." She took a sip of her beer. "Listen, mister, if you want mooseburgers, you go shoot a moose. But I want it delivered to the house frozen and in patty form. Now, before you tell me about your very busy day, enlighten me about the music."

Meg had a good ear for music although her only training consisted of a couple of classes of music appreciation and several years of choir singing under the direction of yours truly.

"*The Dream of Gerontius*, an oratorio by Edward Elgar written around the turn of the last century. His *magnum opus*, if you will."

"Sounds serious. That tenor is working hard."

"Well, he's on his deathbed. Tenors never die quietly. Fear not, fair one. He'll be dead by intermission."

"Then?"

"Then his soul sees God, is judged, and ends up in purgatory."

Meg laughed. "A happy ending then."

"Well, it's not exactly Amy Grant, but it has a certain charm."

"Anything happening at the church?"

I raised my eyebrows. "You should know. You're the senior warden."

"Yes, but I like to get my intel from my spies."

"Nothing new," I said, digging into Meg's famous potato salad. Potato salad was always preferable to chips and cole slaw. Also, my earlier vision of Swiss cheese had been replaced by the reality of extra-sharp cheddar. I was right about the onions, though.

"I talked with Father Tony this afternoon. He said you talked him into staying until the fall, but only part-time. He's making plans for his second retirement. The congregation's going to have to step up and take some pastoral responsibility until we get another full-time priest."

Meg nodded and swallowed a dainty bite of her burger. "Has Bev found anyone to do the Christian education job?"

I shook my head. "Not yet. I think she interviewed someone last week, though. The problem is that the position doesn't pay very much. Not enough to move for, anyway. It'll probably have to be someone from Boone. We've run out of volunteers."

Bev Greene was the church administrator. Father Tony Brown, our "retired" and much beloved ex-priest, agreed to assume the reins until the building project was complete, but only on a very limited basis. That is to say, he promised Meg that, if he was in town, he'd come in on Sunday morning, dust off one of his old sermons, and preside over the Eucharist. When he wasn't in town, we'd have to schedule a morning prayer service. Until there was a new rector at St. Barnabas, the vestry had put Bev in charge of the day-to-day operations and that included hiring a new Christian ed director. St. Barnabas hadn't had a lot of luck with that particular position in the past.

"And the organ?"

I smiled. "Almost there."

"Have you decided what to play on the first Sunday back?"

"Not yet. Whatever it is, I can guarantee it'll be loud."

•••

The next morning, I stopped by Eden Books to pick up a copy of *Crogan's Vengeance*, a graphic novel that I'd ordered for Moosey's birthday. It came highly recommended and purportedly featured pirates, a good story and some first rate cartooning. Moosey spent all of his time in the classroom drawing (much to his teacher's dismay) and currently had a fascination with all things piratical. School was out for the summer at the end of the week, and I figured the book was just the ticket.

Eden Books had been taken over by Georgia Wester when the former owner, Hyacinth Turnipseed, was sent to the state lockup in Raleigh. She'd pled guilty to "depraved indifference to human life" and "mutilation of a corpse" in a plea agreement that sentenced her to five years. She'd be out in three, but she wouldn't be back to St. Germaine. Georgia bought the existing stock for a song, and since she already owned the building (Hyacinth had been renting the space), she was happy to keep the bookstore open. On this beautiful morning, she was opening boxes and filling a shelf with books by North Carolina authors.

The door buzzer announced me, and she looked up over her half-glasses.

"Morning, Chief," she called.

"Good morning to you."

"Your book came in yesterday. I have it behind the counter. Just a sec."

"No rush," I said. "I don't mind looking around."

In my opinion, the bookstore was much better since Georgia had taken over. When Hyacinth owned it, it had a distinctly occult feel to it—a lot of dragony knick-knacks, crystals, sword and sorcery stuff. It was heavy on Harry Potter and vampire chick lit. Now that Georgia was in charge, there were the best-sellers, of course, but also a good selection of regional fiction, mystery, crime, religion, the classics—everything you'd want in a cozy little bookstore.

The door buzzer sounded again, and Bev Greene came in, cheerier than I'd seen her in some weeks.

"Got one!" she said.

"One what?"

"A Christian education director."

"That's good news," said Georgia, walking behind the counter and pulling my book from its hidden recesses. "Anyone we know?"

"I doubt it. She's from Boone. Her name is Kimberly Walnut. She graduated from Asbury Seminary in Kentucky a couple of years ago, but wanted to move back here instead of taking an associate pastor job in Kentucky. She hasn't found a church since she doesn't want to move, and the Methodist bishop here in North Carolina doesn't want her if she won't go where she's told."

"How old is she?" I asked.

"Forty-seven."

"Forty-seven?" said Georgia. "Seriously?"

Bev nodded. "I think she'll be good, though. She's got some fun ideas. Like, she wants to do a Bible School the week after next. She's got a lot of energy; I'll give her that."

"Well, that's one thing off your list," I said. "Now, how about the big opening service a week from Sunday?"

"It's all falling into place," said Bev happily. "June 11—St. Barnabas Day. A big service with the bishop in attendance and then a celebration in the parish hall. The ladies are cooking. Meg can make a speech..."

"I think she'll pass on the speech," I said. "But you can ask her."

"And then we'll open the time capsule."

"I can't wait for that!" said Georgia.

The "time capsule," as it had become known, had been discovered by one of the workmen soon after the demolition of what was left of the old, burnt structure. The engineers had decided that the foundation, although it had done its job for a hundred years, didn't meet the current building codes. In the ensuing excavation, a construction worker came out of the hole with a metal box, about a foot square and eight inches deep, with a small padlock on the hasp. The workers wanted to open it immediately, but Billy Hixon had been walking by and commandeered the box in the name of the church. It had apparently been buried beneath the church during the construction of the second building, probably in 1901, and therefore assumed to be some sort of "time capsule" containing artifacts from a generation long gone and maybe a message to their

22

congregational great-great-grandchildren. Everyone decided that it would be "just the thing" to open the box after the opening service in the new sanctuary.

"It sounds as if you have things well under control," I said, handing Georgia fifteen dollars. She counted out my change, and I stuck the book under my arm and headed for the door. Bev might have things under control, but my problems were just beginning as I walked out onto the sidewalk and into the summer morning.

Two white, fifteen-passenger Ford Econoline church vans had just pulled up in front of The Ginger Cat. "New Fellowship Baptist Church" emblazoned on the side in red block letters identified the owners, and "Follow Me To Jesus" in fancy script across the back doors gave tailgaters a reason to stick tight. The van's engines rattled to a stop in concert, and thirty retirees piled out, dragging their poster-board placards behind them. The signs had obviously been hastily prepared—hand lettered with magic markers and stapled to yardsticks.

"Good morning, Brother Hog," I said, greeting the driver of the first van and obvious leader of this elderly congregation.

"Chief Konig," he said politely, sticking out his hand.

Brother Hog—Dr. Hogmanay McTavish—was the pastor of New Fellowship Baptist Church. He'd begun his ministry as an evangelist and was quite successful, never venturing into the somewhat dubious world of TV evangelism, but preferring the old-fashioned tent-revival as his oeuvre. He had grown plumper since I'd last seen him, but his trademark hairstyle, unique to preachers and used-car salesmen, employed one of the finest comb-overs it had ever been my pleasure to ogle. It began behind his right ear, swung up and around his brow like a magnificent gray halo, then circled his head twice before terminating in a burst of tufts that protruded from the middle of the nest like sprigs of ashen grass; all this held in place by enough hairspray to stick a poodle to a brick wall. Unwound and unstuck, Noylene and I suspected his hair was a couple of feet long and something to behold. Noylene had tried to get him into the Beautifery for a firsthand look, but to no avail.

Brother Hog had come to NFBC as the second interim pastor after Brother Jimmy Kilroy was murdered during the baptism of Kokomo, the talking gorilla. The *first* interim pastor was the church's district apostle, Apostle Jerome, but he could only stay for a few months before he had to get back to his circuit. Brother

23

Hog had come in and taken charge and, after a few months, had decided that being settled was a whole lot easier than putting up and taking down a circus tent every week. In addition, he reported that "scripture chickens"—large chickens that Brother Hog used to choose the passage on which he would base his message—were becoming harder to train. Hog blamed it on the additives that big companies were putting in the chicken feed. "Those chickens are just getting dumber and dumber," he told me. "They got big breasts, but no brains. I tell you, it's a metaphor for our society." I had to agree.

We shook hands as the passengers gathered their possessions from the vans and congregated on the sidewalk.

"What's all this then?" I said, in my cheerful-yet-stern Andy Griffith police voice.

"We've come to protest," said Brother Hog. "Did you see this?"

He held up the morning copy of the *St. Germaine Tattler*. The headline read "Liquor Sales on the Lord's Day—Yes or No?"

"No, I haven't seen it," I said with a sigh. "I thought the paper was just going to list the referendums on the ballot for next week."

"It was," said Hog. "But Jethro Batch—he works at the *Tattler* on the layout desk—happened to read the referendum while he was working on it and brought it to the attention of Calvin Denton, who, as you know, is the editor. Both of these fine gentlemen attend New Fellowship."

I nodded. I didn't know Jethro, but Calvin had been a parishioner at St. Barnabas before he had been hit in the head by a pigeon during an ill-advised Pentecost re-enactment and had used a bunch of his "golfing words" in church. His wife had decided it was time to try another denomination.

"I don't know what shenanigans the mayor is trying to pull," said Brother Hog, "but we are *opposed* to liquor sales on Sunday. It's bad enough we have liquor sales at all. But Sunday? That is just beyond the pale. It seems to me the City Council was trying to sneak this by in a referendum that no one would bother to come out and vote on. I assure you, this is no longer the case."

"Yeah," I said. "I figured something like this would happen."

"We've come to protest, Hayden," said a white-haired woman whom I know only as Miss Ethel. "We have a right to protest. It's guaranteed in the Constitution."

"Absolutely," I said. "But you'll need a permit." I pointed to the police station on the other side of the square. "Lieutenant Parsky will be happy to help you."

"We'll go and get it, Brother Hog," said Miss Ethel. She and another lady toddled off in the direction I'd pointed.

"Thank you kindly," called Brother Hog after them.

The rest of the elderly mob had divided, half going into the bookstore to check out the latest issue of *Mature Digest*, the other half peering through the window of The Ginger Cat at the alimentary knick-knacks that were inviting but unattainable, at least until the restaurant opened for lunch.

"Are all these folks members of your church?" I asked.

"Heavens, no," said the minister. "I made some calls, then went around to several churches this morning and collected our concerned citizens." He held up his fingers as he counted them off. "Sinking Pond Baptist, Melody Mountain Baptist, Brownwood Pentecostal Holiness, Maranatha Four-Square Church of God With Signs Following, and a few folks from Sand Creek Methodist. We've been making protest signs for about an hour."

"I notice that all your protesters are of a certain age," I said.

"Retired folks. Everyone else is working, but we'll have a good group out in force on Saturday."

"Who are you going to picket?"

"We thought we'd picket the mayor's office, but then we found out she doesn't have one," said Brother Hog with a smile. "Then I thought, who stands to gain by beer sales on Sunday?"

"And?"

"The answer is obvious. The Bear and Brew. They're the only establishment open on Sunday that would have any reason to sell liquor."

"So you're going to picket the Bear and Brew?"

"We'll be having prayer meetings outside until they change their mind about wanting to serve liquor on the Lord's day."

"Okay," I said, "but here's the deal. You stay on the other side of the street and you don't interfere with any customer who's going in or coming out of that place of business. You do, and this protest is finished, and I'll lock you up until the election's over. Do we understand each other?"

"We understand each other perfectly," said Brother Hog with a happy grin. "We've got the Lord on our side on this one."

Chapter 3

"I've got news," said Marjorie promptly at 6:48.

Choir practice, during our exile, had been scheduled on Thursday nights, a departure from our traditional Wednesday evening routine, but the St. Germaine chapter of *Shopaholics Anonymous* had first dibs on the courthouse rotunda since they'd been meeting there on Wednesdays for a few years. Rehearsals were moved to Thursdays at 6:30 which meant that Marjorie's proclamation was right on time, just barely preempting my own second announcement that we needed to get started.

"Noylene Fabergé-Dupont is pregnant!" Marjorie said with a flourish.

"What?" said Georgia, aghast.

"What?" said Meg, equally aghast.

"Noylene's *what?"* said Bev, not sure she heard correctly.

"She's *what?"* said Rebecca.

"You heard me," said Marjorie, smiling the smile of the cat that ate the Pentecostal pigeon. "I heard it from Mr. Christopher." Her voice dropped to a conspiratorial level. "He's Dr. Dougherty's nurse's yoga instructor's interior decorator, and she told him that Noylene was due in November."

"Maybe he misunderstood," said Fred from the bass section. "Maybe her bill is due in November."

"He didn't misunderstand," sniffed Marjorie. "I know of what I speak. The wonders of the grapevine shall not be besmirched."

"But I thought they weren't having any kids," said Elaine Hixon.

"Because Wormy's her cousin," added Bev.

"Eeew," said Tiff, from the back row of the alto section.

"Wormy told me he was incontinent," said Mark Wells. "No... that's not right. *Impudent.* He said he was 'impudent.' Something about volunteering for medical experiments down in South Carolina."

"Guess he's not impudent no more," said Varmit Lemieux. Varmit was married to Muffy Lemieux. They both worked out at Blueridge Furs, Varmit as foreman and Muffy as secretary. Muffy had a good voice, but couldn't manage to get that Loretta Lynn twang out of her country soprano. Varmit came to choir practice to keep an eye on Muffy, as did most of the rest of the basses. Muffy was a redhead of singular comeliness and since the calendar had rolled over into June, had exchanged her signature tight angora sweaters, in various pastel shades, for her summer look: tight short-sleeved angora sweaters in various pastel shades.

"How old is Noylene, anyway?" asked Elaine.

"Forty, I think," said Phil.

"Not that it's any of our business," Meg added demurely.

"Well, I'm sure she and Wormy are very happy about it," said Bev.

"Yes," I said. "They're very happy. Now let's look at the Psalm for Celebration Sunday. It's in the back of your folders."

"Have you met the new Christian education director?" asked Steve DeMoss.

"She prefers to be called the Christian *formation* director," said Bev. "It's the new church-speak buzzword."

"Yes, I've met her," I said. "Kimberly Walnut."

"And?" said Steve.

"She seems uncharacteristically qualified," I said. "Brilliantly so."

Bev jumped in. "And while we're on the subject, I'm supposed to make an announcement. We need to enlist volunteers to help out with the Bible School program the week after our celebration. It'll take place in the late afternoons behind the church in the garden. It'll be fun!"

"But more about that after rehearsal," I said. "The Psalm..."

"Where's our detective story?" asked Muffy. "You promised."

"It's on the back of the Psalm," I said, my shoulders slumping. "But you can read it later. Could we maybe sing a bit?"

"Well, what are we waiting for?" barked Elaine. "Get cracking! We're not here for our health, you know!"

•••

By the time Meg and I arrived home, it was close to nine in the evening. Too late for a big meal, but on Thursdays we always had a late lunch at the Bear and Brew and then had a snack when we came in from choir practice. A snack followed by a drink. Sometimes two, depending on the rehearsal.

Meg always arrived home first. We were in separate vehicles anyway, and I had to lock up the courthouse where we'd been holding choir rehearsals. While Meg rooted around in the fridge, I fed Baxter, put a dead baby squirrel outside on the window sill for Archimedes, and wandered into the den to put on some Mozart to cleanse my aural palate. Symphony 39 in D Major. The majestic introduction with accompanying brass fanfares filled the house, and I sat down at the typewriter.

Meg came in a few minutes later with a braunsweiger and onion sandwich on toasted Russian black bread and a cold bottle of Ommegang Abbey Ale. She set the plate on the side of the desk.

"Sorry," she said, with an apologetic kiss. "We're out of Old Thumper."

"Old Thumper is good," I said, "but *this* is the perfect beer to drink with a braunsweiger and onion sandwich on the first day of June."

She settled onto the couch, first setting her glass of red wine on the coffee table in front of her, then cradling her plate in her lap and tucking her legs beneath her on the soft leather cushions. "I called Noylene on the way home. She's pregnant, all right."

"I take it that this is a surprise?"

"Oh, yes," said Meg. "When they got married, both she and Wormy thought he was, in her words, 'shootin' blanks.' Of course, that original test was twelve years ago."

"I thought he got re-tested right after the wedding."

"That's what he told us. He needed to get the loan for his Ferris wheel."

"I remember," I said. "He put his sperm count down as income. Ah, those were heady days for borrowing money. Getting a loan was as easy as lying to your banker." I took another bite of my dinner. "This is a great sandwich. Really!"

"Glad you like it," said Meg with a smile. "But don't talk with your mouth full."

Yep. I was married.

•••

Buxtehooter's was always bustling on "Two-Dollar Thursday." The Baroque sing-alongs had been relegated to Friday and Saturday nights since the big brawl on Pachelbel's birthday, so the crowd was less rowdy than usual, but the beer-fräuleins were still hustling buckets of two-buck suds delivered primly on jutting chests the size of Myron Floren's accordion. The owners had put a TV over the bar and tuned it to the local religious network -- a mixture of shows that included "Are You Smarter Than A Lutheran?," "Dancing With the Baptists," and "CSI: Vatican." It drew a small crowd. Unitarians mostly.

I grabbed a seat at a table and whistled at Ermentraud, my current favorite Buxtehooter's soubrette. She sashayed over in a dirndl packed as tightly as the coach section of a 747.

"Hiya, Erms," I said. "Gimme some tonsil varnish and put a head on it."

"Ja, ja!"

"And maybe we can meet later? When you're off work?"

"Ja, ja! Ich werde Sie hinter den Abfalleimern treffen, meine mollige Gans. Ich freue mich darauf, Ihr Geld zu nehmen."

I got the "Ja, ja" part, smiled, and tucked a sawbuck into the bouquet of bills that sprouted from the top of her blouse like some kind of hydroponic, milk-fed cabbage patch. It's good to be a detective.

•••

"Nice," said Meg, reading over my shoulder. "And by 'nice,' I mean terrible. What does the German mean?"

"You'll have to look it up, *meine mollige Gans*," I said.

"I'm not sure I like the sound of that," said Meg. She descended gently back onto the couch and picked up the biography she'd been reading. That was the thing about Meg. She never flopped. She never plopped. She descended, she alighted, she settled gracefully. It was marvelous just to watch her exist.

"How is the protest going at the Bear and Brew?" she asked, without looking up from her book. She licked the tip of her finger and used it to turn a page.

I took my beverage over to the couch and plunked down beside her. Unlike Meg, I plunked.

"Brother Hog is true to his word. He's been holding a prayer meeting every morning all week long, and no one has bothered any of the patrons. So far, so good. The Bear and Brew is even letting the old people use their bathrooms."

"I think that's sweet," said Meg. "It's good to have a civilized demonstration."

"But Saturday, there'll be a whole lot more people. Most of Brother Hog's congregation has been working during the meetings. On Saturday, they'll be off work and out in full force."

"I'm sure you and Nancy can handle it, dear," she said, reaching over and patting me on the cheek, her eyes still scanning the words on the page in front of her.

"You know who one of the owners is?" I said, trying to draw her out of Raymond Chandler's life story.

"Russ Stafford?"

"*What?* How did you know that?"

She put her book down and laughed. "He's been in on it since the beginning. A silent partner. I'm his accountant, remember?"

"No, I didn't remember."

Russ had been a high-roller, a real-estate developer before everything went south. After his most ambitious development, The Clifftops—a gated, golfing community eighteen miles from town—went belly-up, he'd gone to Asheville to see if he could make a living selling cars. He could and did. Russ was a born salesman. Within a few months, he was back on top, had moved back to town, and had been concentrating on his real-estate business. Even with the downturn in the economy, we all knew Russ was doing well. He was well-liked, smooth as a well-shaved eel, and along with his wife, Brianna, had even started chaperoning the St. Barnabas youth group. Together with another couple, Gerry and Wilma Flemming, they hosted a Sunday night youth get-together at their respective homes that the Staffords had christened Afterglow.

"Not only didn't I remember you were his accountant, but I certainly didn't know he had an interest in the Bear and Brew."

"I think he owns sixty percent," said Meg. "Something like that. Francis Passaglio has a smaller share. They don't do any of the day-to-day stuff, though. Why do you think the youth group gets all those pizzas at half price?"

The Bear and Brew had begun life as a feed store in the 1920s. The new owners had kept the heart-pine floor boards; the tin signs advertising tractor parts, chicken feed, windmills and most everything a farmer could want from a mercantile; and the ambiance that comes with an old store that had seen four generations gather around the pickle barrel, swap stories, play checkers, and whittle untold board-feet of kindling. It had good, sturdy tables, wooden chairs, and an old 1950s juke-box in the corner, the kind that played 45's. There was still just the hint of saddle soap and leather in the air, but mostly what the Bear and Brew had was pizza. Good pizza and good beer, a bar and a couple of sixty-inch plasma televisions. The owners thought they could sell a lot of beer on a Sunday afternoon when the Carolina Panthers took the field or if North Carolina, or Duke, or Wake Forest, or any one of a hundred other college teams was shooting hoops.

"Well, either way," I said, "it'll all be over next Tuesday, and we can get back to normal. As normal as we get."

"Have you seen the weather forecast?" asked Meg. "We're supposed to get a squall on Saturday. It should be a doozy. One of those summer thunderstorms."

"That could be a blessing in disguise. The protesters might stay home."

"You should be so lucky," said Meg.

Chapter 4

Saturday morning loomed like a movie special effects spectacular, something out of *Twister* or maybe *Lord of the Rings, Part Two*. I woke at 7:30 to the sound of distant thunder—not just the occasional clap, but the rolling kind, the kind that comes in waves that make the windows rattle, the thunder that makes you think that maybe there are bowling alleys in heaven and makes you wonder if angels have their own bowling shoes or if they have to wear rentals. But maybe that's just me.

We had our windows open, and, until this morning, the weather had been pleasant and cool. Now the air was warm and heavy and uncomfortably sticky. I gave Meg a kiss, left her to her Saturday morning dozing and headed for the kitchen to make some coffee, closing the windows along my trek through the house. Archimedes, sitting primly on the kitchen counter, greeted me with two great blinks as I walked in. He hadn't been around for a few days, but he sensed the storm and obviously preferred waiting it out in the house. I didn't see Baxter, but knew he'd probably taken refuge under the bed in one of the guest rooms, his usual place during a thunderstorm. Fearless in most circumstances, Baxter was a sissy when it came to thunder. I started the coffee, then went outside to the garage and fetched a couple of mice out of the fridge for the owl. Coming back in, I saw some towering thunderheads toward the southwest, huge clouds with puffed edges standing straight up. The overshooting top, that cauliflower-like bubble of cloud that peeks out of the flat top of the thunderhead, told the story. This was going to be bad. The clouds were gray and menacing and were lit almost continuously from inside by diffused lightning. The storm was still a long way off, though. I judged fifty or sixty miles.

I went back inside, fed Archimedes his breakfast and took a cup of coffee to Meg. She was sitting up in bed watching The Weather Channel.

"Thanks," she said with a smile, then nodded toward the television. "The storm is over Kingsport. High winds, hail, and a lot of lightning."

"Eighty miles away," I said. "I thought it was a little closer than that."

"It's big. Should hit us around noon."

"Yep," I said. "I'm going to go for a run, and then I've got to get into town. I'll get breakfast at the Slab."

"I'll come with you," said Meg. "Not running. Breakfasting."

"Great," I said. "I'll be ready in an hour."

"Me, too," lied Meg.

•••

The Slab Café was packed. Meg and I had figured that the crowd would be sparse, thanks to the big storm a-brewing. Luckily for Pete, Brother Hog had made the Slab Café the rendezvous point for all the protesters. And since everyone was rendezvousing anyway, why not have some breakfast? Every table was full, every barstool occupied. Luckily for us, one of the tables was occupied by Pete and Cynthia, and they'd saved a couple of seats.

"Wow," said Meg. "I had no idea the Slab was this popular."

"Oh, yes," said Pete. "Hog brought in a couple of vans full of customers, and then some came in on their own." He pointed to the corner by the door. About thirty protest signs were stacked neatly against the wall.

"Who's flipping the flapjacks?" I asked.

"José's back there cooking. Wormy's washing dishes. Noylene's got the floor, and Pauli Girl should be here shortly to help out. I called her about a half-hour ago when I saw what was happening."

Noylene scuttled by and splashed our coffee cups full in a mad dash to the kitchen. "Be right back," she called over her shoulder. "Y'all want waffles, right?"

"Well, actually..." said Meg, raising a finger in a futile gesture and looking in desperation at the swinging kitchen door. It was too late. Noylene was gone.

"Right," said Cynthia. "Waffles for everyone."

"I'll have mine with waffles," I said.

"That storm is gonna wash these guys out," said Pete. "They'd better get to praying pretty quick. If they wait too much longer, they're going to be soggier than Noah's houseplant."

The cowbell hanging on the door banged with a jangle, and Pauli Girl raced to the kitchen to clock in and get her apron on. Noylene appeared a few seconds later with an armload of orders. The folks in the Slab on this dreary morning were not of the tourist variety

33

and so were not at all antsy about getting fed in a hurry. They had plenty of time.

The four of us, as well as the other patrons, had our repasts in front of us and were well on our way to feeling mighty satisfied by 9:30. Belgian waffles with maple syrup, whipped butter and walnuts on a summer morning in early June just can't be beat. In fact, it was 9:30 on the nose when Brother Hog opened the front door, stuck his head into the Slab and called, "It's time to start! Let's get moving, folks!"

Everyone, except the four of us, got up, collected their slickers, purses, umbrellas and placards and made their way to the cash register where Noylene was stationed.

"It's like music to my ears," said Pete wistfully, as we listened to the register ding every time the drawer opened. "The register and the cowbell. Someone should write a concerto."

Fifteen minutes later, the Slab was shed of customers, and the tables were piled high with dirty dishes. Noylene and Pauli Girl came out and fell, exhausted, into a couple of chairs at the next table. They were joined by Wormy and José, who came out of the kitchen a moment later.

"Thank God *that's* over," said Noylene. Pauli Girl nodded her agreement.

"I think they'll be back for lunch," said Cynthia. "At least that's what I heard. Some of them anyway. They think The Ginger Cat's too expensive, and they don't want to go into the Bear and Brew since they're picketing it."

"That's just good manners," said Meg.

"Well," said Pete, getting to his feet, "we'd better get this place cleaned up and ready for lunch, then."

"They may be back here earlier than that," Cynthia said, with a glance to the front windows. "Look outside."

In the last thirty seconds, the sun had all but disappeared, the air pressure had dropped noticeably, and the trees were starting to wave their branches in a somewhat alarming fashion.

"Lookit my arms," said Pauli Girl, holding her arm out for inspection. "All the hair's standing up."

"Weird," said Noylene.

"I'm takin' my break," said Wormy, helping himself to a waffle that had been mysteriously left uneaten on a moderately clean plate.

"Me, too," said José. He didn't make a move for a waffle, but did get up and pour himself a cup of coffee.

"I'll go see how the prayer meeting's going," I said.

"I'm coming, too," said Meg. "For a little while, at least."

"Count me in," said Cynthia.

Pete gave Cynthia his best puppy-dog look. "I thought maybe you'd help out here," he said. "Look at this mess."

"Nope," said Cynthia. "You're on your own. I'm the mayor."

•••

By the time we'd battled the wind and walked across the park, the vigil was in full swing. Brother Hog was standing on a soapbox— an actual soap box. I don't know where he got it. I wasn't sure I'd even seen one before. On the side of the wooden box was the old Ivory Soap logo accompanied by the slogan "99.44/100 % Pure: It Floats." Brother Hog was perched on top, his comb-over struggling valiantly to remain atop his head. The rest of the crowd, forty or so people, huddled together against the upcoming storm. The giant storm clouds had rolled in, and the rumbling of the thunder was beyond ominous. The flashes of lightning that we saw were still hidden in the folds of the great clouds, but they were frequent and not a little frightening.

"I'm not going to stay out here very long," said Meg.

"Me, neither," I said.

The Bear and Brew wasn't open, and no one would even be there for another half-hour or so, but Russ Stafford joined us on the sidewalk behind the faithful gatherers.

"I sure hope that referendum passes," he said. "It'd be good for business."

"I have no problem with it," I said. "I certainly wouldn't mind a beer with my pizza on a Sunday afternoon."

"Now you all know why we're here," said Brother Hog in a stentorian voice. He hadn't been preaching at tent revivals all those years for nothing. He had the lungs of a Wagnerian tenor.

"We don't need to be serving any liquor on the Lord's Day. That day is set aside for the worship of God in His Holiness. Now, we can't do nothin' about how people choose to spend that day. Many will go to sporting events. Many will choose their own relaxation over the worship of God Almighty. Can't do nothin' about that. But we *can* do something about this, and what we *can* do, we *should* do."

"Amen, brother," came a voice from the crowd.

"So, let's pray that God will intervene in this election and that His will be done."

The wind had finally gotten hold of the end of Brother Hog's hair, and it was unwinding at a rapid pace. He didn't see it until it came floating by his face on its second revolution, at which point he grabbed the end and stuffed it down his shirt. Most people didn't notice or didn't care. They had their own well-being to worry about.

"Let us pray," yelled Brother Hog, over the wind. A huge clap of thunder made everyone jump. It was close.

"Dear God, all powerful and ever living King of the Universe..."

We felt the first raindrops. No. Not rain. Hail. The wind picked up, and a few umbrellas went inside out with a whoosh. About half of Brother Hog's congregation made for shelter.

"We ask that you, in your might, and by your power, stop this unholy act of irreverence by whatever means that you see fit. We ask that you allow your sovereign people to observe your Holy Day without the influence or temptation of alcohol and that this establishment,—" he stabbed a finger at the Bear and Brew— "be fated as Sodom and Gomorrah was fated in days of old."

"That's a little harsh," yelled Russ, struggling to be heard above the wind. "The Bear and Brew is hardly Sodom and Gomorrah."

"He's just getting wound up," I hollered back. "It's the revivalist in him."

Another clap of thunder, nearer still, got the remaining faithful looking around worryingly.

Brother Hog continued, now shouting above the storm that seemed about to break all around us.

"Grant our boon, O God, and in your power, show Your will, Your Holy and Righteous will, to the inhabitants of St. Germaine, that they might know and fear the LORD!"

It was at that moment that the lightning struck, a sheer bolt of blinding light that illuminated the clouds and hit so near us that the explosion of sound was simultaneous, and we could feel the electricity snap in the air. Half a beat later, there was an explosion, then another, and the whole roof of the Bear and Brew burst into flames.

We learned later that the lightning strike, in that mysterious way that lightning sometimes travels, had managed to negotiate a path from a roof vent to the storage room behind the kitchen and ignite the five-hundred gallon natural gas tank that fueled the pizza ovens. We didn't have any municipal gas service in St. Germaine, and everyone that used gas, either for heat or for cooking, had their natural gas delivered and pumped into their storage tanks at regular intervals. Some of these tanks were buried in the backyard, marked by a silver metal dome that jutted six inches above the soil, but most sat on blocks behind people's houses. A few businesses, like the Bear and Brew, had the tanks inside.

The volunteer fire department was on the scene fifteen minutes after the fire started, but they were ineffective at best. The building was a total loss; the back half of the roof had fallen in moments after the trucks had driven up. Besides, the firefighters couldn't possibly have poured more water on the fire than the storm itself was providing. It was as though God blew up the building, then decided to put out the fire, just to show that He could.

Meg, Russ Stafford, Cynthia, and I had backed into the Appalachian Music Shoppe, a smallish store just across from the Bear and Brew, to get out of the weather. Ian Burch, the proprietor, a musicologist trying to eke out a living selling replicas of medieval and Renaissance instruments, had been in the back when the explosion happened, but came running to the front window as the sound of the blast rattled some of his shawms and recorders off their shelves.

Brother Hog and the protesters disappeared a matter of moments after the supernatural event. The ones who had come to the prayer meeting by church van piled back in quicker than you could say "Mene, mene, tickle the parson," and the vans were long gone by the time the fire trucks pulled up. The folks who had their own cars walked quickly away in the manner of children who realize that something they've been involved in has suddenly gone very wrong. It was like when you were a kid, and you and your friends would dare some other kid to throw a firecracker at Old Lady Porter's cat, and when he did, the "pop" made Mr. Whiskers dash into the road where a moving van flattened him, and everyone walked away, stiff-legged, as fast as they could in different directions, hands in pockets, trying to look as inconspicuous as possible. Most of *these* folks went to find a store where they could lie low, wait out the heavy rain, and pretend they hadn't been involved.

I'd asked Russ if there had been anyone inside the restaurant, and he indicated that the building had been empty.

"No one comes in before ten," he said through clenched teeth. "We open at noon. Well," he added, "we used to."

"Maybe it's not a total loss," suggested Cynthia.

As if in answer to Cynthia's observation, the rest of the roof fell in with a crash that we could hear over the rain and behind the closed glass door of the Music Shoppe.

"Wow," said Ian Burch, in his high, squeaky tenor, having collected his assorted rauschpfeifes from off the floor and set them back on the shelves. "It's sort of like that preacher called down the wrath of God upon the Bear and Brew."

I looked over at Meg. She raised her eyebrows in return.

"That fat, little son-of-a-bitch," Russ growled. "I'll sue his damned pants off. Him *and* his church."

"You have insurance, don't you?" asked Meg.

"I'm not gonna file a claim," said Russ. "New Fellowship Baptist Church is responsible. New Fellowship Baptist Church is gonna pay."

Chapter 5

Celebration Sunday had awakened under a quilted blanket of fog, low-hanging tracts of "smoke" that gave the Smoky Mountains their unique character as well as their name. This was the Appalachians in June. At the intervals where the smoke vanished from the headlights, the hills in the lower gaps were awash in color. Meg and I drove slowly down the mountain, taking our time, not just because of the fog, but because the wildlife was plentiful and unconcerned by traffic. We slowed for a family of deer—a doe and two fawns—that had decided that the flowers beside the road would make a perfect breakfast. They looked up, startled, as we drove past, then dove into the purple blossoms of the rhododendron. By the time we arrived in town, the sun had managed to chase most of the fog back into the hollers, and the day was looking as the celebration and welcoming committee of St. Barnabas thought it should.

We'd rehearsed in the new sanctuary for the first time on Wednesday evening. Moving our rehearsals back from Thursday evening to Wednesday hadn't helped our sight-reading any, but we were out of the courthouse at last and glad of it. The choir loft, still situated in the back of the church, had been outfitted with new chairs, music racks for folders, new hymnals—the works. The organ wasn't quite finished, but most of the ranks were there and functional, having been voiced and tuned late in the week. I was playing the Bach *Little Prelude and Fugue Number 4 in F Major* for the prelude and had even managed quite a bit of practice in the last week. The choir had been working on *Behold, the Tabernacle of the Lord* by William Harris, perfect for the first Sunday back in our new church and one of the choir's favorites. In addition, there was new service music, three hymns, the Psalm, and *Sicut Cervus*, the lovely Palestrina motet, to be sung during communion. It would be a full day.

I was in the church office, making copies of my latest literary effort and a couple of easy hymn descants to pass out to the choir, when Kimberly Walnut, our brand new Christian formation director, walked in.

"Good morning, Hayden Konig," she chirped, rattling her single piece of paper as if to say, "If you're going to be using the machine

39

for a while, I'm really in a hurry, so you should get out of the way and let me go first." I wasn't buying it.

"Good morning, Kimberly Walnut," I replied. The photocopier chugged away happily. "I hear you have quite a Bible School planned for next week."

Kimberly saw that she wasn't going to get to the copier any sooner, gave a disgusted huff through pursed lips and crossed her arms in annoyance.

"Yes," she said. "It's a program I did with a large church in Kentucky when I was in seminary. It's called Bible Bazaar 31 A.D. It's all centered around a bazaar in biblical times. The kids all dress up. The adults as well. We do plays and skits about stories in the Bible and help the kids do activities. You know, like sandal-making and carpentry and pottery and baking and things like that. We didn't have enough time to do it all ourselves, so New Fellowship Baptist and Sand Creek Methodist are going to join us. We should have quite a turnout."

"Sounds great," I said. "Meg and I signed up. I'm the tax-collector. I think Meg is one of the tent-mothers."

"Meg said you'd write our creation play. Is it finished yet?"

"She said *what?*"

"She said you'd be happy to write our creation play. It's for the second day."

I sighed. The photocopy machine finished its chore with a final click, and I retrieved my papers from the tray.

"I'm sure it will be great. I've heard good things about your writing," said Kimberly. "Now, if you don't mind, I'm *really* in a hurry."

•••

Two hours with Ermentraud (and thirty bucks) later, I found myself back in the office picking potato skins off my slicker and avoiding accusing glares from Marilyn, my secretary.

"You had two calls," she said, tossing a couple of slips of paper onto the desk. Marilyn was a dame with more angles than curves, more spunk than smarts, and a Yugo. She looked at me from behind cheap dime-store glasses with eyes that looked as though they were being piloted by tiny mice in swivel-chairs.

"Yeah? Any potential clients?"

"One girl's on the way up," Marilyn sniffed. "I told her you'd be back by three so she made an appointment. The other guy wants to sell you some insurance."

"Tell him to buzz off," I said. "I ain't interested."

"I'll tell him," said Marilyn with a huff and a twirl, a half-eaten jelly donut suddenly appearing between her lips. She snorked at it delicately. "And it looks like your appointment is here."

I just had time to settle behind my desk when the knock at the door came rattling across the room. I looked up at the dame lolling in the doorway; a broad with more curves than a Möbius algorithm in which $x(u,v) \neq (1 + \frac{1}{2}v \cos \frac{1}{2}u)$, and I was hooked like a carp with a mouthful of chicken guts. So I did what any shamus worth his slide-rule would do. I fell in love.

She batted her peeper-shades at me, then, ballerina-like, rose gracefully en pointe, extended one slender leg behind her like a dog at a fire hydrant, and curtseyed. She seemed to have an ecclesiastical halo around her head as she made her way across the carpet in that particularly sexy way of walking which was really due to a partially slipped disc and incipient arthritis.

"My name is Constance," said the apparition. "Constance Noring. And I need your help."

•••

"Brilliant!" said Georgia, once the choir had gathered for our pre-service warm-up and rehearsal.

"Awful," said Meg.

"Awfully brilliant," I admitted. "Now, my dear wife, please fill me in on my volunteering to write a creation play for the Bible Bazaar."

"Oh...umm..." Meg bit the end of her finger in consternation and did her best to look chagrined. "Did I sort of forget to mention that?"

"Where's my music?" said Marjorie. "Someone stole my music!"

"Besides," said Meg, "if the lovely Constance Noring is any indication for your writing prowess, you should be able to knock out a creation play in a couple of minutes."

"Hey! Did you hear?" said Phil Camp. "Russ Stafford filed suit yesterday in District Court," The basses were still milling around and trying to find their seats. "He's suing the Baptist Church."

"I expect that Judge Adams will toss it out," said Bob Solomon. "Anyway, Russ should just go ahead and file an insurance claim."

"He mentioned that he'll go that route if he loses his lawsuit. The insurance company says they'll be glad to wait and see what happens."

"I guess they will," answered Bob. "They might not have to pay off at all."

"Palestrina," I announced. "Then the Harris anthem. Sit up straight and sing it like you mean it."

•••

As services went, this one was a doozy. Bishop O'Connell, in fine form and full regalia, Father Tony Brown in his new vestments, the acolytes, lay-readers, choir members, and Eucharistic ministers, all followed our champion thurifer, Benny Dawkins. Benny walked behind the crucifer who was proudly holding the church's new brass and silver processional cross aloft, and the group entered in all possible pomp and pageantry. Benny Dawkins had finally realized his life's ambition by actually *winning* the International Thurifer Invitational, held in Santiago, Spain, last summer. He wasn't a long-shot to come out on top, by any means, having finished as one of the top-five thurifers for the previous several seasons, but the competition seemed to be going the way of his arch-rival, Basil Pringle-Tarrington, who was a sentimental favorite due to his losing an arm in an unfortunate incense-pot training exercise with his sensei in Japan. Benny, never one to be cowed by sentiment, took the competition right to Pringle-Tarrington, first stunning the judges with his new signature move, *St. Moulagh's Breastplate*, a maneuver that left a startling vaporous vision of a Celtic cross hanging in the air above the altar before dissipating a moment later, only to be replaced by a phantasmic image of the Keys of St. Peter. The gasps from the crowd were gratifying enough, but nothing compared to the spontaneous weeping that followed as Benny turned and faced the crowd, whirled the thurible in front of him until it became a blur of gold, and the sheer speed of it made the glowing coal light the pot from within until it shone with a radiance matched only by Benny's serene expression, then walked back down the aisle through a fairly reasonable smoky depiction of Da Vinci's "Last Supper." Pringle-Tarrington withdrew from the competition; many thought his spirit had been broken, and he'd never compete again.

I couldn't see the magic Benny was performing this morning since I was playing the prelude when he came in, but there was appreciative applause as he censed the altar, made his turn and headed out the door to the sacristy. Our bishop didn't care for incense—it made him sneeze—so Benny used special hypoallergenic smoke and got out of the nave as soon as he'd done his part.

The new organ was splendid, the choir sang exceedingly well, the bishop's sermon was well-received, and the congregation even sang the hymns. Father Tony had banished the dreaded "children's moment" soon after he'd returned to taking charge of the services. Now the kids follow the crucifer out to a special children's service during the second hymn and come back in for communion.

Moosey and his gang were there, five ten-year-olds who struck terror in every Sunday School teacher that had ever had the pleasure of teaching a class on Noah's ark while simultaneously trying to corral two of every reptile native to the St. Germaine ecosystem—reptiles that had been courteously provided by any one and possibly all of the afore-mentioned gang. Moosey, Bernadette, Ashley, and Christopher had recently added a fifth to their confederacy, someone to take the place of the departed Robert, a casualty of the seductive appeal of New Fellowship Baptist's *Golgotha Funpark*. His name was Dewey.

The "Children of the Corn," as they were known by the Christian education department, had been deemed too old for children's church and so now congregated on the back pew where they spent the service passing notes and looking up all the smutty parts of the Bible they could find.

"Balaam sat on his ass," giggled Ashley during the sermon, passing the pew Bible to Bernadette and pointing out the offending passage.

"You kids be quiet now," hissed one of the ushers. "Or I'll make

43

you go sit with your parents." This admonition always worked for about two minutes.

The service ended on a high note, Karg-Elert's *Nun Danket Alle Gott*, that rattled the dentures of several old folks who'd neglected to use a sufficient amount of Polygrip, as specified in the prayer book. The choir applauded enthusiastically, and we shed our vestments and headed down to the new parish hall for brunch, speeches, and the opening of the St. Barnabas time capsule.

"I'd like to welcome everyone here today," said Bev Greene, once everyone had gotten their food and found some seats. "This is a very special occasion."

"Balaam sat on his ass," snorted Moosey, finally looking at the piece of paper he'd been passed during the sermon.

"Hush," said Meg, snatching the paper away and sticking it in her purse. Ruby, Meg's mother, took Moosey's hand, and we found our table, our reservation being held by Nancy and Dave who had come over for the festivities, then sneaked into the parish hall during the final hymn to beat the crowd. Nancy, in her police uniform due to a specific duty she'd agreed to perform during the opening of the time capsule, managed to hold our seats by looking daggers at anyone who attempted to usurp them. It was an effective tactic, and people shied away, looking for a less inhospitable landing.

"It's particularly appropriate," said Bev, "that we have our Celebration Sunday on the feast day of St. Barnabas, and thanks to all the workers, contractors, and everyone else who has been toiling around the clock to make sure we were ready for our homecoming. They've done a beautiful job rebuilding our church, and we're more grateful than words can say."

Applause.

We went through several short speeches, including one by Mayor Cynthia Johnsson; our chief architect, Jessica Adeline; Michael Baum of the Baum-Boltoph Organ Company, and Father Tony, with Bev acting as the mistress of ceremonies. Meg had declined the invitation to be included.

At long last, Bev yielded the dais to Bishop O'Connell, who stepped up to the mic, all smiles and hairspray, his lilac shirt a little damp from the perspiration that a service clad in extra-fancy vestments, a thirty pound cope and a velvet-lined mitre tend to encourage, especially in June.

"It is my pleasure, as always, to be with the congregation of St.

Barnabas," said Bishop O'Connell. "I know you don't want to hear another sermon by me..."

Laughter.

"...and so I shall be happy to turn the program over to Billy Hixon. I'm sure we're all waiting to view the contents of the time-capsule that was found under the foundation of the old church. However, before we do, let us have a prayer."

Every head bowed, and the bishop said the collect for St. Barnabas Day.

"Grant, O Lord, that we may follow the example of your faithful servant Barnabas, who, seeking not his own renown but the well-being of Your Church, gave generously of his life and substance for the relief of the poor and the spread of the Gospel; through Jesus Christ our Lord, who lives and reigns with You and the Holy Spirit, one God, for ever and ever. Amen."

"Amen," the crowd answered.

"Billy?" said the bishop, gesturing to Billy Hixon, who climbed the two steps onto the low platform, carrying the box that everyone had come to see opened. There was a small side-table set up in the middle of the platform, and Billy placed the box on it. The box was exactly thirteen and one quarter inches wide, twelve and a half inches long and nine inches deep. Billy had measured it. It was black in color, made of steel and quite heavy. On the front of the box was a hasp, also made of steel, and a brass padlock that had been cleaned. The lock had the date 1875 stamped into the brass along with the manufacturer's information—the Handy Lock Company of Pittsburgh, Pennsylvania. Nancy now followed Billy onto the dais. She had two items with her. The first was a set of shims. (One of Nancy's hobbies was picking locks.) A lock this old, she reckoned, shouldn't give her any problem at all. She figured it would take thirty seconds, a minute at the outside. Failing this, Billy had made sure that she also had a pair of bolt cutters. Even though it would be a shame to cut the antique lock, everyone had come to see the contents of the box, and the celebration committee didn't want anyone to go away disappointed.

"This here's the box that was found under the foundation when we were digging for the new basement," said Billy. "We think that it might be a time capsule, but we don't know for sure. It was probably put in the ground around 1901. According to the records in the courthouse, that's when the foundation was completed for the second church. There could be anything in this." Billy picked up the box. "Greetings from Sunday School classes, bulletins, church documents, old pictures…"

"Shake it, Billy," came a voice from the crowd. "See if it rattles."

"Nah, I ain't gonna shake it. But it's time to open it up."

The excitement was palpable, and people chattered enthusiastically. Billy set the box back down on the table and gestured toward Lieutenant Parsky. Nancy was as good as her reputation. As a hush fell over the crowd, she bent down, chose a shim from her case, and, twenty-three seconds later, the lock dropped open. A cheer went up from the congregation. Nancy blushed, waved, and came back to our table. Billy slid the lock off the hasp, opened the box and lifted out a leather pouch, about the size of an old marble bag we'd all carried as kids, cracked and stiff with age. He set the pouch on the table, reached back into the box and brought out a plain white envelope. He opened the envelope and unfolded a letter.

"Read it aloud," called a voice, as Billy skimmed the contents of the letter and looked somber.

"It's from Father Simon Faulks," said Billy.

"I remember the name," Meg whispered to me. "His picture used to hang in the hallway with the other priests who had been rectors of St. Barnabas. He must have been the priest when the old church was rebuilt."

I nodded in agreement.

"The date at the top says 21 November, 1900."

The crowd had become very quiet.

"I can't read this," said Billy.

"Sure you can," called someone. "Just read it."

"I mean I *can't* read it. It's all old-time cursivy and stuff."

"I'll read it," said Ruby, standing up. "I'm old enough to remember good penmanship." She ascended the platform, and Billy handed her the letter.

"To whomever finds this," began Ruby. "I don't know how this story will end, nor even how it began, and I ask the Almighty's forgiveness if I've erred in judgment."

I am Rev. Simon Faulks, rector of St. Barnabas for five years and in office at the time of the terrible fire.

Before taking my vows, however, I studied geology at the university, was granted a degree, and was subsequently employed by the Piedmont Mining Company, for whom I worked for several years. I only disclose this information to explain why I believe that it was God's Holy will that I, a humble man of faith, yet of particular background and education, be here in St. Germaine at this particular time.

We laid dynamite for the foundation on Tuesday last. The entire town came out to enjoy the spectacle and the noise, and, although some children got a bit close, the explosions went off without incident and a fine time was had by all. On Wednesday, before the laborers arrived, I took it on myself to go into the pit and poke around. The geologist in me, I suppose. What I found was nothing short of astonishing.

Ruby asked for a glass of water, took a sip, set it on the table behind her and then continued.

Resting lightly on the rubble were gemstones. Raw diamonds. I collected nine in the hour I spent in the pit. These matched thirteen other stones I had found in a cave on Quail Ridge one month earlier. I have sent those thirteen stones to a colleague in Charlotte for confirmation. The nine I found here, I leave in this box.

I never looked again. These were days of trial for St. Barnabas, and the discovery of a diamond mine at the site of the church would have demanded more temperance than I believe the church, or even the town, could have exhibited. St. Germaine would have followed the hasty progress of so many boomtowns, and I saw the ruination of everything we'd worked to accomplish.

And so I keep my secret. God forgive me if I've done wrong.

Yours very truly,
Fr. Simon Faulks

Ruby looked at Billy, who was holding the leather draw-string bag. He worried it open and, after a long moment, poured the gemstones into his hand. Nine unassuming rocks, the size of marbles, tumbled out and rested in his outstretched palm.

"Are they big?" asked someone from the back.

Billy shrugged. "Don't look that big to me, but I don't know nothin' about diamonds. I'll take 'em into Boone and see what's what."

"Quail Ridge," said Nancy. "That's Noylene's place."

"Yep," I said.

Chapter 6

Meg was spending the night at her mother's house. I took this as an opportunity to smoke one of my Cuban cigars, put on my new recording of Mahler's *Rückert Lieder*, and try out a new beer, Sprecher Black Bavarian Style Lager, that Pete had picked up in Asheville. I settled behind my typewriter, listened to the bass voice of José van Dam fill the house, then slipped a piece of paper behind the platen, gave a few clicks and started writing.

•••

"My name is Constance," said the apparition. "Constance Noring. And I need your help."

"I can help," I said. "It'll cost you two Cs a day plus expenses."

"I don't have that kind of money," she suddenly blubbed, turning on the waterworks, like that guy who, you know, turns on Niagara Falls for the tourists every morning. "My mother's living at the bus station and she needs her medicine..."

"Knock it off, sister," I grunted. "You're not talking to some schlemiel with a heater who doesn't keep score. I know exactly who you are and why you're here."

The tears dried up as fast as Hillary's campaign contributions and were replaced by eyelashes flapping so hard I could feel my nose-hair beginning to part.

"Now how would you know that?" she mused, musing in a bemused fashion.

I reached into my desk drawer and pulled out the July issue of <u>Hymns and Hers</u> magazine. It fell open to page 64, and there she was, in all her peeled and pagan glory, directly across the page from the article on the use of the dudelsack in Lenten services. Constance Noring. Diva. Miss July. Originally from Australia. Turn ons: Long walks on the beach, snuggling, Reformation hymnody, Philip Glass concert arias, dispensationalist theology, and puppies.

"I see you have it bookmarked," she said, grinning like the puppy that ate the dudelsack. "Maybe you'd like a first-hand peek?"

"Maybe I would, toots. Maybe I would."

•••

The next morning, I found Billy Hixon in the parish hall, sitting at one of the tables, having a cup of coffee with Meg, Elaine, and Bev. Meg gave me a smile that I could feel down to my toes. I walked up and returned her smile with a smooch. A loud one.

"Oh, get a room," said Elaine, rolling her eyes in mock-disgust.

"Yeah," added Billy. "What if Elaine and me made out every time we saw each other?"

"Probably do you two some good," said Bev. She held up her empty cup and gestured toward the coffee pot. I took the cup from her hand and walked over to our new, state-of-the-art, industrial coffee maker.

"Grab a cup for yourself, too, and pull up a chair," said Bev.

Billy would be outside mowing as soon as the dew evaporated and the grass was dry enough for his crew to begin. Billy Hixon's lawn service took care of the grounds as well as most of the other lawn care and landscaping concerns in St. Germaine. The two big contracts that kept Billy's service afloat during the long winter months were with the city and included Sterling Park and Mountainview Cemetery. Wormy DuPont had opened his own cemetery when it became clear that Mountainview was "sold out." If you didn't already own a resting place and wanted to be planted in St. Germaine, your only choice was Woodrow DuPont's Bellefontaine Cemetery, known locally as Wormy Acres. Wormy offered all the latest in perpetual accoutrements, including *Eternizak*, music piped underground into your coffin for all eternity, or at least until your credit card expired.

"I'm going to have to raise my rates," said Billy. "We've got that whole meditation garden to take care of now."

The original garden had been small and unimpressive—little more than a fenced patio with some boxwoods placed somewhat inartistically along the edges of the concrete pavers; but the garden had been expanded, and its renovation included as part of our

50

rebuilding process. There had been an old, dilapidated house on the lot behind the church, but Thelma Wingler had left it to St. Barnabas when she died, and the vestry had decided to tear the house down and use the space for a meditation garden. Now it encompassed more than an acre and was landscaped to take advantage of the mature dogwoods, poplars, and maples that Thelma never had the heart to tear down, even though they had grown huge and were too close to her house.

"Fine," said Bev. "I agree. Just give me a written quote. I'll pass it on to the senior warden, and we'll see what she has to say."

Billy turned to Meg. "So, what do you say?"

Meg took a sip of coffee. "I haven't seen the quote, but I'll tell you one thing. Give me the real price. Not that one where you add ten percent and then give it back to the church as your tithe."

"I never did that!" said Billy. "Well...not for a while."

I pulled out a chair, sat down, and joined the conversation. "Well, what's the verdict?" I asked Billy. He looked at me blankly. "The diamonds. Remember?"

"Oh, yeah," said Billy, brightening. "Real. Absolutely. I called over to Appalachian State early this morning. The head of the geology department put me onto a gemologist who teaches at Lees-McRae College. I met him at 8:30 this morning."

"And?"

"He couldn't tell for sure until they're cut, but he figures four to seven carats of finished stones. Maybe twenty to thirty thousand, depending on the quality and how they're cut."

"Wow!" said Meg. "I didn't think they'd be worth that much."

"St. Barnabas gets richer," I said. "I'm going to have to start taking a salary. Twenty thousand, eh? That's a lot of money."

Billy and Bev laughed. Meg hid a smile behind a sip of coffee.

"Hayden," said Elaine. "Twenty to thirty thousand *per stone*. Nine stones. You do the math."

•••

"Something's wrong," said Ardine.

The afternoon shadows were creeping over the gravel drive and had almost reached the stoop of the old trailer, a 1972 vintage single-wide mobile home, now looking its age. I'd come by the McCollough homestead to pick up Moosey for Bible Bazaar 31 A.D.

"It's been going on for the past couple of weeks," she added.

Ardine had been a pretty woman in her youth, but had led a hard life up in the hills. Now her face was thin and lined, and her graying hair was pulled back into a bun. She wore a loose, shapeless, cotton dress, handmade probably, and had her hands tucked into the pockets of a large cardigan sweater. She looked perpetually cold and rarely smiled.

"What has?" I asked.

"I don't know, but something happened to Pauli Girl. She won't tell me what, but I've been through this myself, and I know something happened."

"You think someone's bothering her?" I asked.

"Worse than that," said Ardine. "I've seen it before. Hell, it happened to me!"

I nodded, waiting for more information.

"She came home from that youth group meeting at the church two Sundays ago. Afterglow, they call it. She wouldn't talk or nothin'. Just went into her room and closed the door. Then, when I asked her about it the next morning, she just clammed up. She never went back, either."

"You think it's one of the boys?" I asked, running the roster of boys that might be in the youth group through my head.

"No," said Ardine, with finality. "Pauli Girl don't have no problem with boys. Not that age, anyway. She's a good girl and sure of herself. She'd laugh them to scorn or put a knee where it'd do some good if one of them ever bothered her."

I waited.

"No, it's somebody else. An adult. She acts like she's ashamed, but it ain't her fault."

I raised my eyebrows. "She never went back to the youth group?"

Ardine set her mouth in a hard line. "Nope. And she loved it."

"You want Nancy to talk to her?"

"I want Meg to talk to her."

"You know who it is, don't you?" I asked.

"I'm pretty sure. You need to find out."

•••

Bible Bazaar 31 A.D. was taking place behind St. Barnabas Church in the new garden area. Kimberly Walnut had scripted a three-day activity, taking place from four to six o'clock. Two hours of biblical fun. There were canvas canopies pitched all around the park beneath the poplars and the maples, and the garden was a beehive of activity. Children were busy being divided into the twelve tribes of Israel and being assigned tent-mothers and teenaged helpers from the youth group. They were diving into their costumes, pillowcase-like tunics with holes for their arms and heads and cinched around the waist with a rope or a colorful piece of cloth. In the far corner, a "temple" had been set up—a white funeral tent with plywood pillars in the front and benches inside for the services. In another corner of the park was the drama area where the skits were scheduled to take place. There was a four foot high "well" made out of stacked stone pavers in the center of the garden. An old wooden bucket sat on its lip.

Meg was already in her outfit, something very fetching that she'd gotten from Morocco. Not exactly biblical, but she sure won the prize for best looking tent-mother. She was busy dropping muslin sacks over the heads of squirming and excited children, but gave me a wave when she saw me. Moosey scampered over to her tent and disappeared in two blinks.

Cynthia was there, her belly-dancing ensemble tinkling with every step, happy to do her part as mayor. She was scheduled to have a belly-dancing class with the little girls after they'd strung enough beads and bells together to make some noise. I didn't have the heart to tell them that belly-dancing, in days of yore, was the purview of prostitutes and wanton women.

Jeremiah the donkey was in a pen, along with a couple of sheep and Seymour Krebbs' camel. Seymour was in attendance, too, holding the lead rope and wearing a faded blue bathrobe, a bath towel draped over his head and tied with a belt, and sandals with black socks. Father Tony was wandering around dressed as the high priest, complete with a long, false, gray beard. He'd be officiating at the temple service. Ian Burch had also been invited, being the only one in the area with his own shofar, a ram's horn that was being used to call the children to the temple for the daily service and to the drama area for scheduled performances. Ian also had the wherewithall to make the horn sound like something more than

53

a flatulent donkey—something we already had, judging from the space the children were giving Jeremiah.

The activity tents were manned with adults from all three of the churches—St. Barnabas, Sand Creek Methodist, and New Fellowship Baptist—all ready to lead the children in pursuits they essentially knew nothing about but were happy to learn along with the kids. I recognized most of the folks, but there were some who were new to me.

Shea Maxwell was helping at the sandal-making tent, Carol Sterling was getting the clay ready to be molded by young potters, and Gerry and Wilma Flemming, the herbalists, were putting fresh-cut herbs in mason jars. The herbalists were also in charge of making tea for the tent-mothers and had an electric coffee pot burbling away to provide hot water on demand. An orange extension cord snuck out the back of the tent and snaked its way to the parish hall.

Brianna Stafford was sorting the beads in the jewelry shop, and Beaver Jergenson, the armorer, would happily show the little warriors in the group how to make some basic biblical armor out of wood, leather straps, and scraps of metal. There was a candy shop where the children could spend a coin if they had one left over. They'd get their ten coins each morning from their tent-mother, and coins were required for apprenticing in the shops, petting the animals, giving alms to the beggars, making their offerings in the temple, and various other things.

Skeeter Donalson made a convincing leper, although, with all the dirty rags he was wearing, it was tough to make out his pockmarked face and permanently greasy hair.

In addition to the folks from St. Barnabas, there were some I didn't know—a basket weaver, a carpenter, and someone who, according to the placard in front of her tent, was named Lydia, and was going to show kids how to dye cloth purple. I also didn't know the two soldiers or the beggar. Their costumes were great, though, probably left over from an Easter pageant at one of the other two churches. I was the Roman tax collector and, hence, the bad guy.

Kimberly Walnut was scuttling back and forth like a hermit crab at the Dead Sea, checking her lists and directing adults to their appointed posts. She looked very busy, but, in fact, the tent-mothers had everything under control. Kimberly just had to get the skits running on time.

Unfortunately, the first person I ran into after I'd gotten into my tax collector outfit was Pete. This particular costume was more along the lines of John Wayne's centurion look in *The Greatest Story Ever Told*. Short red tunic with a "pleather" overlay replete with brass-colored plastic medallions on strips that hung past my waist, sandals, and a red cape. There was a helmet as well. It was a bit small, but it more than made up for it in style, the hard plastic silver crown sporting hinged face-guards, and topped by red bristles stiff enough to sweep the floor of the Slab Café. The sword was a bonus.

Pete almost fell over laughing. "Your legs!" he guffawed. "You need to get down to Noylene's Dip 'N Tan."

I stabbed him with my sword. Unfortunately, it was made of rubber.

"Did you bring my sandwich?" I asked.

"Yep." Pete handed me a paper bag, still chuckling. "As ordered. One Reuben sandwich—corned beef, sauerkraut, Swiss cheese and Russian dressing on toasted rye."

"And chips?"

"Yeah. Chips."

Moosey ran up, followed closely by Christopher and Dewey. "Hey, Chief!" he yelped. "Lookit! We're in the tribe of Issy-something!"

"Issachar," said Christopher.

"We're the warriors!" said Dewey.

"Robert's over in the Baptist tent," said Moosey. "He has to stay with his class. He's a Benjamin."

"I could use some Benjamins," said Pete.

"Bernadette and Ashley are in our tent, too," said Dewey, after giving Pete a blank stare for a moment. "And Samantha."

"We coulda had two more," volunteered Christopher, "but Mrs. Konig said six were plenty."

I smiled at the mention of Meg's moniker. She'd gone back to her birth name, Farthing, after her divorce ten years ago, but decided that she'd rather like to be a Konig. Fine with me.

"I expect you six are plenty for anyone," I said.

"Can I see your sword?" asked Moosey.

"Nope. I'm the tax-collector. I'll be expecting some coins from each of you."

"Mrs. Konig said our coins were for the shops," said Christopher. "And I already gave one to the leper."

"Right," I replied. "But I'm the Roman tax-collector. And the tax man always gets his share."

"Not if you can't find us," said Moosey. He pushed his glasses up on his nose and gave me a crooked grin. Then he and the two boys took off like a shot and disappeared into the crowd.

•••

I spent most of the two hours walking around the bazaar, giving glaring looks to children who'd already gotten the word and who screamed whenever I showed up. Not exactly according to scripture, but precisely what I wanted to do every time I signed my tax return in April. I noticed Moosey and the rest of the tribe of Issachar, including the girls, over at Beaver Jergenson's armorer's tent for most of the afternoon.

There were two skits taking place on the first day, the first scheduled at five o'clock and the second just before closing at six— *The Conversion of St. Paul* and *Peter's Dream*. At the scheduled time, the shofar sounded and all the kids ran over to the drama area and plopped down on the grass. I missed the first play, deciding instead to rendezvous with a certain tent-mother who kept giving me come-hither glances and was looking far too tempting in her coral-red Moroccan djellaba.

"Forbidden love," she whispered, with a seductive smile. "And with a Roman centurion. How naughty."

"Aren't you afraid of reprisals from your people?" I asked, moving closer.

"No. Just from my husband."

"Hmm."

"Close the tent flaps, my brave centurion," she giggled.

Hence, I missed the first play, but I couldn't miss the second one, having been assigned a dramatic role due to the fact that I was the only one with the correct costume. After St. Peter, ably portrayed by Benny Dawkins, had described his vision in which a voice commands him to eat a variety of impure animals with the admonition "Do not call anything impure that God has made clean," I walked up, was converted and subsequently baptized. My part was easy. I had to answer "Yes" to Peter's question, "Do you accept Jesus Christ as the Son of God and will you be baptized?" then kneel down and be sprinkled. This rankled the Baptists to no end, but, as Kimberly Walnut pointed out to them, it was just a skit and besides, we didn't have a river handy.

After the second skit, the kids hied back to their tents for clean-up, costume turn-in, and refreshments. Other than the donkey having some digestive problems, the afternoon went without incident, and a good time was had by all.

Chapter 7

The front-end loader and two backhoes made short work of what remained of the Bear and Brew. They'd worked for a few hours on Monday afternoon, knocking everything down, and by Tuesday, when I arrived in town, they were filling two large dump-trucks with rubble. The trucks would have to make a few trips, but I figured that by noon, all that would remain of the restaurant was a flat slab of cement.

I walked over and watched for a while, then walked back across the park and stuck my head into the police station.

"Anything going on?" I asked.

"All quiet," said Dave. He was behind the desk reading the *Tattler*. "Have you seen this morning's paper?"

I shook my head, and he held up the front page for me to see. The headline read "Missing Diamond Mine Discovered In St. Germaine."

I sighed. "I'm going to get some breakfast."

"Hang on," he said. "I'll come with you." He folded the paper and dropped it on the desk. "I already talked to a reporter from Raleigh. They're picking up the story. The news should be all over the state by tomorrow."

"That's great," I said. "Just great."

"Look on the bright side," said Dave. "Just think of the folks that'll come into town to shop. Let's see. They'll need pickaxes, backpacks, burros..."

I laughed. "Seen Nancy this morning?" I asked, as we made the corner and walked the half-block to the Slab.

"Not yet."

"I guess she'll know where to find us."

•••

We'd just settled into our breakfast of country ham, grits and scrambled eggs when Russ Stafford barged in the door, followed a moment later by Nancy. Russ sat down at the counter after making a quick survey of the occupants of the café. Cynthia dashed into the kitchen to pick up an order, so Nancy grabbed a coffee cup off the counter, poured herself a cup, and made her way over to the table.

Her plate was waiting at her place when she arrived.

"Aren't y'all sweet!" she said in a voice that made us reach for our steak knives.

"What?" asked Dave.

"Aren't y'all sweet to get me a plate?"

"We always get you a plate," I said with a wary look. "What's the deal?"

"There's no deal," she said, sitting down next to Dave and helping herself to the family-style breakfast. "Sheesh. I was just trying to be pleasant. My therapist said I should attempt to be a bit less caustic."

"Well, stop it," said Dave. "It's creeping me out."

I nodded my agreement, and released the grip on my knife.

"Hey, Pete," Russ called into the kitchen. "*Pete!*"

Pete came out of the swinging kitchen door, wiping his hands on a towel. It was obviously his morning on the grill and he was wearing the better part of a Spanish omelette on his apron. His baseball cap served to keep his ponytail under control as well as proclaiming his loyalty to the Tampa Bay Rays.

"Yeah?" he said, tossing the towel onto the counter. "What's up, Russ?"

"You seen Noylene?"

"She's off this morning," said Pete.

"Well, she's not at home," said Russ.

Pete shrugged. "So? Have you checked over at the Beautifery?"

Russ got to his feet and looked around impatiently. "I need to talk to her. If you see her, tell her I'm looking for her, will you?"

"Sure," said Pete.

Russ walked out and banged the door behind him. Pete watched him go with a shake of his head.

"That's the second time he's been in this morning," he said as he walked up to our table. "The first time, he grilled Cynthia for about ten minutes."

"Must need to see Noylene," said Dave, through a mouthful of grits.

"Brilliant detective work, Sherlock," said Nancy.

"I thought you were going to be a bit less caustic," said Dave. "You might have hurt my feelings."

"I tried it. Didn't work."

59

"Glad to have you back," I said.

The cowbell clanged against the glass door again, and Wormy walked in and sat down at the counter where Russ had been just moments before.

"Was Stafford looking for Noylene?" he asked.

Pete and I looked at each other, then back at Wormy.

"Yep," said Pete. I took a sip of coffee.

"He's been up at the double-wide," said Wormy, his eyes narrowing. "I seen him up there twice since Sunday talkin' to Noylene. I was in the woods and seen him. He was up there last month, too. One time, Noylene even asked him inside. He's up to something. I knows it."

"Maybe he's trying to find out about the diamond mine on Quail Ridge," said Pete.

"That'd be my guess," I said. "He's a real estate developer. Maybe he's trying to buy the ridge."

Wormy shook his head. "She won't sell it. Been in the family for years. And anyway, I've been all over that ridge since Sunday. If there's a cave, I can't find it." He stood up, walked to the front door, then turned and looked at our table. "I'm keepin' my eye on him. That Russ Stafford's a snake or I ain't a capon."

We watched him exit and head off in the same direction as Russ.

"I expect he *is* a snake," said Cynthia, having come back in from the kitchen and hearing Wormy's declaration. She pulled a chair up to our table and sat. "But what's a capon?"

"A rooster, I think," I said.

"Now, tell me about those diamonds."

"They're real," I said, "and worth a small fortune. The interesting thing is this."

Nancy and Dave stopped eating in mid-mouthful and looked at me in anticipation.

"You all know," I started, "that there are all kinds of gem mines up here in these mountains. The most valuable gems that come out of them are rubies and emeralds, but there's also amethyst, citrine, topaz, garnets—a whole lot of stuff."

"How about diamonds?" asked Pete.

"According to the geologists, there should be, but the only diamonds that have been found in North Carolina are now in a museum in Charlotte. Thirteen of them. No one knows exactly where they came from, but people have been trying to find out for over a century."

"You're kidding? Thirteen?" said Pete.

"Coincidence?" asked Nancy.

"I hardly think so," said Cynthia. She looked thoughtful for a moment. "So, other than under St. Barnabas, the only other place in North Carolina that *might* have diamonds is up on Quail Ridge."

"Or so says the Rev. Simon Faulks," I said.

•••

At 3:30 in the afternoon, the crowd behind the church was already starting to gather. Bible Bazaar 31 A.D. was gearing up for the second day of revelry. I met Meg in front of the tent of Issachar. I hadn't donned my centurion outfit yet, but I still had an hour or so before I needed to start terrorizing the children.

"I talked to Pauli Girl," said Meg. "There's definitely something going on, but she won't say what. All that she would say was that she wasn't ever going back to Afterglow."

"You think she's being sexually harassed?" I asked.

"Or worse. She's not even seventeen yet. What if it's one of the adults?"

"That's what Ardine thinks."

Meg looked over toward the shops. "There're only two sets of adults involved with the youth group. Russ and Brianna Stafford and Gerry and Wilma Flemming. Could be one of the older boys, I suppose."

"Ardine says that Pauli Girl wouldn't have a problem with any of the boys."

"Well, tread lightly, my dear," Meg said.

"Could you talk to a few of the other girls in the group? On the sly?"

"I can try."

•••

Ardine brought Moosey to the church since she'd volunteered to work in the bead tent. Bud tagged along as well. I spotted him walking toward the animals.

"Bud!"

He turned to me, and a smile lit his face. "Hi, Chief. You need a wine recommendation?"

"I can always use some advice," I said with a grin, "but let me ask you something first." I lowered my voice and my smile faded. "Did Pauli Girl say anything to you about the youth group?"

Bud shook his head, then looked puzzled. "No, but she's been awful quiet for the past week or so."

I scratched my chin and decided to change the subject. "Well, how about a delicious red wine for Saturday night? Meg's fixing a pork roast with garlic and rosemary. Roast potatoes, maybe some homemade applesauce."

Bud closed his eyes and thought for a moment. "I know just the thing," he said finally. "But it'll cost you. It's about sixteen bucks."

"I can just about swing that," I said.

"It's called *The Tillerman* from Hook & Ladder, a California winery. Vintage 2003. It's a mixture dominated by Cabernet Sauvignon, but also has Cabernet Franc and a jolt of Sangiovese. It's a soft, easy-going wine, but the Sangiovese grape adds a spicy element that sort of enables it to fit just right with rosemary-infused pork."

I had pulled out my pad and jotted all this down while he was talking. It was always good to have a pad handy when Bud was giving wine advice.

"A 2005 Jacob's Creek Riesling would be good if you'd rather have a white," Bud continued. "It'll be better than a Chardonnay. It's got some zesty acidity in the finish with just a hint of apple on the palate. With a side dish of applesauce, it would be great!"

I kept scribbling. "Uh, huh. Zesty acidity. Apple. Got it."

"A third choice would be a red called *Rubesco* Rosso di Torgiano. Get the 2001. It's from the Lungarotti vineyards. *Rubesco's* only available as an import, though. I think that the Sangiovese-based wines pair well with pork. They have a dry, almost dusty finish, and the light body and plummy fruit flavors are almost chutney-like, and underscore the intrinsic sweetness of the meat."

I finished writing and snapped my pad closed. "Excellent!" I said.

"You'll let me know how that comes out?" asked Bud. "I'm keeping notes."

I had to remember that Bud, despite his encyclopedic knowledge of wine, didn't actually drink it. Oh, he'd sip with the best of them, but then he'd spit it right back into the spittoon. He'd also spent hours helping out in the kitchen of The Ginger Cat, sampling every herb he could find and finally sniffing the aromas of each dish before it left for the tables. His nose was never wrong.

"I'll let you know," I said. "Thanks!"

•••

An hour into the second day of Bible Bazaar, Kimberly Walnut found me shaking down an eight-year-old girl for two coins and an unleavened bagel.

"Where are your actors?" she asked in a panic. "Your play starts in three minutes."

"Oh, sorry." I took a bite of my bagel as the little girl ran off. "We're ready. Let me round up the cast."

"I can't wait to see it," gushed Kimberly, positively ebullient. "I just love this story. Adam and Eve and the Garden of Eden and the rainbow and everything."

"Right," I said. "Although the rainbow doesn't show up until Chapter 7."

The play, or rather, the *vignette*, featured my friend Will Purser, an acting teacher at Lees-McRae College, and Mr. Christopher Lloyd, the interior decorator from Boone I knew could never pass up a good role and a chance to dress up in angel wings. I'd enlisted Moosey and his crew as well. They were to stand in front and announce the days. The crowd gathered and sat on the grass in anticipation of an inerrant interpretation of the story of creation.

"Day one!" shouted the kids, not exactly in unison.

"This is the beginning," roared Will in his biggest and most omnipotent voice.

Will had explained to me that playing the part of Yahweh is always a tough gig and there are a couple of different schools of thought. One is to understate the character and portray the Almighty as an approachable, loving grandpa, sort of like George Burns. The second is to go ahead and pull out all the stops and make him more of a thundering, James Earl Jones, pillar-of-fire type of guy. Since Will had the voice for it, I'd suggested the latter.

"No, no, wait..." said Will. "Change that. In the beginning..."

"But, Boss, we've been around for some time now," said Mr. Christopher, looking quite resplendent as Gabriel in his Victoria's Secret angel wings.

"They don't know that," replied God. "This is going in the book. In the beginning... Write that down. Got it?"

Gabriel: Like I'm going to question the Deity. I've got it, I've got it. What are you up to, anyway?

God: This is my divine plan. And don't bother me right now. I'm creating a world.

Gabriel: I hope it turns out better than Saturn.

God: I thought the rings were a nice touch, but the helium atmosphere made all the angels sound like Mickey Mouse.

Gabriel: Who?

God: Never mind. Now, let's see. We'll start with a formless void and darkness over the face of the deep. And now ... (watch closely) ... LET THERE BE LIGHT!

Gabriel: COOL! You never did that before!

God: Heh heh...Tomorrow I'll clean this mess up. Divide the waters from the heavens, that sort of thing. Day two is always easy. Put some names on this stuff, will you? You know—Day, Night—the usual. Write it up and leave a copy on my desk. You know... I think it's pretty good.

"Saturn?" said Kimberly Walnut who was standing next to Meg. "*Mickey Mouse!?*"

"Day three!" announced the chorus.

God: I think I'll put a fig tree over there in the corner.

Gabriel: OK. One fig tree.

God: And some asparagus. I love asparagus.

Gabriel: Got it. We need to hurry up. You have an appointment with Mister Fancy Pants Angel-Of-The-Morning at six.

God: Who do you think you're talking to here?

Gabriel: Not that I meant to rush you or anything.

God: Good. Now about that ragweed...

64

"What?" said Kimberly Walnut. *"Asparagus?"*

Meg pretended not to notice.

"Day four!"

God: SUN!

Gabriel: Good choice.

God: MOON!

Gabriel: Nice...nice...

God: STARS!

Gabriel: Could use a few more in my opinion...

God: MORE STARS! BILLIONS OF STARS! UNLIMITED GALAXIES OF STARS! AN EVER-EXPANDING, UNENDING UNIVERSE! Happy?

Gabriel: Yeah. I really like it. By the way, how did your meeting with Lucifer go?

God: Not great. And I'm really beat. Let's call it a day.

"Day five!" The remnant of the tribe of Issachar was doing itself proud.

God: OK. Where were we? Oh, yeah. Fill the water with birds, and fill the sky with fish."

Gabriel: Umm, Boss? We did that over in Alpha Centauri. It didn't work out so well.

God: Oh, right. Let's reverse it this time.

Gabriel: You want me to write all this down verbatim?

God: No. Throw some thous and haths in there somewhere. And make it sound snooty so the Episcopalians will like it. The Baptists will change it back, anyway. Here, try this. "Let the waters bring forth abundantly the moving creatures that hath life, and fowl that may fly above the earth in the open firmament of heaven."

Gabriel: You've sure got a way with words, Boss.

God: That's why I'm God.

"Day six!" shouted the kids.

God: Hmm. What have I forgotten? Elephants, lions, cows, pigs, whales, unicorns...

Gabriel:	That really looks like fun. Could I make one?
God:	Well, OK...there're some pieces over there by the fig tree.
Gabriel:	Let's see, here. What have we got left over? Fur... duck bill...beaver tail...poison spikes...webbed feet. I think I'll make it lay eggs. HAHAHAHA! This is great! I'll call it a...a walrus. No, wait. We did that already. I know...a platypus. What's this in the corner? A pouch! I'll give it a pouch. And Wings!
God:	Nope. I need those wings on this flying mouse.
Gabriel:	Aw, c'mon. You've already got birds.
God:	𝔑𝔬!
Gabriel:	Oops. Hey, no problem, Boss. By the way, who's going to take care of all this stuff?
God:	That's the next part of my plan. Hand me some of that dirt there.
Gabriel:	This isn't the best dirt. There's some better dirt over under that apple tree.
God:	This dirt's just fine—just flick that worm out of there. Now stand back and watch this! *(Whooosh)*

Bud, playing the part of Adam, appeared on the stage. He only had a couple of lines.

Gabriel:	Wow. He looks like you!
Adam:	I'm hungry.
God:	How about some asparagus?
Adam:	Who can we get to cook it?
God:	Hmm. You'd better lie down for a little while.
Gabriel:	Can we get ribs with that?

"And God saw that it was good!" chanted the chorus.
"Amen," said Meg.
"What just happened?" said Kimberly Walnut.

•••

My sword was missing, but I was pretty sure where to find it. I found the tribe of Issachar keeping Beaver, the Armorer, busy with questions and utilizing his expertise in edged weaponry.

"Lookee here," Beaver was explaining to Dewey. "If you make that grip just a little bigger, you can get more force into your thrust. Then your sword will go right through the belly without dinging off the spine."

"Ah, yes," said Dewey thoughtfully. "Yes, I see."

"Where's my sword?" I thundered, in my gruffest centurion roar.

The kids all jumped and giggles broke out all over the tent.

"Hi, Chief!" said Moosey. "You here for our taxes?"

"Not yet," I said, placing both hands on my hips and trying out my best Victor Mature biblical epic pose. "I've come for my sword."

Bernadette giggled again. She was working on a spear about six feet long and topped with a wooden point cut out of a piece of plywood and painted gold. "It's over there," she said, pointing to the corner of the tent. "We just needed to see how it looked."

I walked over and retrieved it. Moosey was wrapping the hilt of his own sword with a leather strap. He had a wooden shield slung over his back as well. Christopher was trying on a leather breastplate with rawhide ties. His dagger was stuck in his belt. Ashley and Samantha both had scimitars, distinctly Arabian in look and more medieval than biblical, but both nicely decorated with painted unicorns and butterflies. Leaning against a table were a few more spears of the type that Bernadette was fashioning.

"Have you girls been over to the jewelry shop?" I asked.

"Nope," grunted Samantha, testing her blade with her thumb.

"Hey!" said Ashley. "I've got an idea! Why don't we put some jewels on these spears?"

"Yeah," agreed Bernadette. "Let's go get some!"

All three girls tore out of the armorer's tent, leaving the boys to their work.

"Where are the other kids?" I asked.

Moosey shrugged. "They came by, but we told them that Issachar was the warrior tribe. I guess they went to make pots or something."

Dewey snorted and looked down, busying himself with his blade.

"Yeah," I said. "I guess that's it."

•••

Seymour had volunteered to give all the kids camel rides, and even two at a time and circling the garden just once, making sure that everyone had a turn, was a tall order. As it was, the last six children around the park might well have thought they'd skipped the Bible Bazaar and inadvertently entered the camel races at Abu Dhabi.

As dramatic quality went, the second skit of the day, *Paul and Silas in Prison,* fell just a little below last month's fourth grade presentation of *Our Tribute to America,* in which Moosey donned a short beard and a stovepipe hat and recited the *The Gettysburg Address.*

Benny Dawkins had switched his persona from last night's St. Peter to the narrator. Paul and Silas were being played by Russ Stafford and Gerry Flemming, respectively. There were two prisoners, judging from their shackles and orange jumpsuits, but I didn't know them. I was pretty sure they were real prisoners because Nancy was standing behind them, her hand resting on the butt of her gun. She saw me and made her way over, skirting the crowd. There was a Roman guard as well, intrinsic to the story, being portrayed by Bud.

"Those your prisoners?" I asked, as Nancy sidled up.

"I just borrowed them for a couple hours. They were on a road crew on Old Chambers, picking up litter."

"They know their lines?"

"They'd better. Otherwise, it's porta-potty cleaning duty for both of them at ASU tomorrow. Hey, did you hear Skeeter got picked up? Drunk and disorderly. He's in lockup in Boone." Nancy shook her head. "Stupid."

"How'd he get over there? He doesn't have a car."

"Wormy was with him."

I shook my head. "Can you go over and check on him tomorrow?"

Skeeter was the town crazy, but we all liked him and tended to look out for him in the way of all small towns. He might be crazy, but he was *our* crazy.

"I'll try to go over around supper time," said Nancy. "He needs to dry out."

I nodded and turned my attention back to the stage. The play was beginning.

68

"Paul and Silas had been put in prison," began Benny. "It was midnight and they were singing songs to God."

"What do you want to sing next?" asked Russ, aka Paul.

"Let me think," answered Silas.

The tribe of Issachar, weapons bristling, marched into view and settled in beside me at the back of the crowd.

Prisoner One: "I don't believe it. How can they sing when they are in prison? Don't they realize they could die tomorrow?"

Paul: "Yes, we do know that, but God will look after us no matter what happens."

Prisoner Two: "It doesn't look like your God is looking after you now."

"You'll see," said Paul slyly.

"Who *wrote* this crap?" asked Dewey, his distaste evident. The rest of the tribe looked disgusted as well.

"I think it was Jesus," said Ashley. "He usually writes this stuff."

"It was *not* Jesus," I whispered. "I think it was Kimberly Walnut."

"The one with Gabriel was way better," said Moosey. The other kids agreed.

"Just then, there was a major earthquake," Benny the Narrator announced. "The chains that tied Paul and Silas to the wall fell off, and all the doors in the prison opened."

All the players fell to the ground in dismay. Bernadette laughed.

"Let's get out of here," said the prisoners in unison, the way people often speak when faced with such an opportunity.

Paul: "No, don't! God wants us to stay here."

Samantha spat on the ground and narrowed her eyes. "I'll tell you one thing. If I was a prisoner, I'd be outta there so fast, I'd look like a roadrunner cartoon."

"Just then the guard arrived," said Benny.

Bud was way off to the side, talking to Ardine, and walking in the other direction.

"Just then the guard arrived," said Benny again, this time louder and looking around for Bud. The crowd tittered. Meg, sitting in the front and looking around, caught my eye and gave me a meaningful toss of her head.

I rolled my eyes, resigned to my fate, and walked through the crowd toward the front. "Oh, no!" I exclaimed. "The prisoners have all escaped, and I shall be killed. Better to die now by my own hand." I drew my rubber sword ominously, intent on the happy dispatch, and sincerely hoping no one would stop me in time.

"Don't harm yourself," said Russ. "We're all here."

Benny studied me for a moment, a twinkle in his eye, then said, "The guard called for some lights and came and checked and the prisoners were all there. Then he knelt down at Paul's feet."

I knew a cue when I heard it. "Please tell me what I must do to be a Christian," I said.

Paul: "You must believe in Jesus, who died and rose again."

And so, for the second time in as many days, I was saved and baptized.

Afterwards, I went over to Meg's tent where the tribe was getting out of their tunics and stashing their weapons.

"You saved the day," she said, kissing me on the cheek. "I don't know where Bud went. He was right there...then he was gone."

"I saw him talking to Ardine."

"It's a good thing you know your Bible stories."

"Yeah," I said. "Good thing."

Chapter 8

Having Constance Noring on my arm was my ticket
to Anywhere, USA. She was a definite 10, a 5 with her
own credit card, and as we made the rounds of the club
scene, it didn't take me long to discover why she needed a
private eye.

"Someone's trying to frame me," she whimpered. "Frame
me like Mandy Lisa's great-aunt Mona."

"Don't try to charm me with similes, Doll-face," I grinned,
chomping down extra-vigorously on a particularly tough
stogie that I'd found, still burning, on the outside window
sill of the downtown Christian Church (Disciples of
Christ). "You ain't got the chops."

We made our way past the usher, the bouncer, the
velveteen rope, and into the Fellowship Hall. I always
appreciated the parenthetical, non-creedal denominations.
Not much liturgy, but the beer was great, and there was
usually a lit cigar on the window sill.

"I thought you liked them," she pouted, her lips
suddenly red and full, like tubes of blood drawn by an
inattentive phlebotomist. "Similes, I mean." Her ample
bosom quivered in the night air like a whale trying to
scratch its back.

"Nah. I can take 'em or leave 'em. Metaphors? Them I
like. Metaphors are gold."

"Humph," she humphed. "Anyway, that detective, Jack
Hammer, wants me to come downtown for questioning."

"I'll bet he does. I could use some answers, too. For
starters, how did you know Wiggy Newland?"

She laughed. A deep, throaty laugh, like that sound the
cat makes just before it throws up a hairball.

"We were in business. I can tell you now since I'm
your client and you're bound to silence by the Liturgical
Detective's Sacramental Seal of the Confessional."

"Uh...yeah," I said, my mind working like a steel trap,
only one that had been left out so long, it had rusted
shut. "That's right. Suuure."

"Diamonds," she whispered.

The silence was so thick you could cut it with a knife--
not even a good knife, but one from that set of Ginsus
you got as a wedding gift; the one you told yourself you'd
return for a $10 Walmart gift card, but in the end, forgot
about because your wife ran off with the maid-of-honor--
that kind of knife.

"Diamonds?" I said.

"Lots and lots," she sparkled.

•••

"I tell you," said Pete, "it's going to be quite a trial if it gets that far. I'd love to be on that jury."

There were a lot of places to eat in St. Germaine, but only one for truly deep theological discussion, and that was the Slab Café. It was at this very table that we discussed the finer points of doctrine, such as whether or not a talking gorilla can give his life to Jesus, why some saints simply refused to decompose, or why tossing pigeons off the church balcony on the day of Pentecost was really not a good idea.

"The way I see it," said Nancy, "Russ doesn't have much of a case." Meg indicated her agreement.

"Au contraire," said Pete. "He's got a *hell* of a case. Brother Hog prayed for God to smite the Bear and Brew, and God did it."

"I have to agree with Pete," I said. "Brother Hog is in quite a quandry. He can argue that he didn't have anything to do with the lightning and that it was just coincidence, but then he'd be saying that God doesn't answer prayer."

Pete continued. "And if God *does* answer prayer, Brother Hog's prayer in particular, then he's responsible, because he asked God to do it."

"*Asked*," I said. "That's the key. If he'd *asked* God to do it, and God had a choice whether to do it or not, then he might be okay. But Brother Hog *called* on the Name of the Lord. Not only that, but he's a Word of Faith preacher, and their theology says that you can ask God whatever you want and believe it, and he'll give it to you. 'And all things, whatsoever ye shall ask in prayer, believing, ye shall receive.' Matthew 21:22."

Meg looked at me suspiciously.

"I did a little research," I admitted.

"So God had no choice?" asked Nancy.

"Not according to Brother Hog," I said. "God is bound by his Word. Within the Word of Faith teaching, a central element of receiving blessings from God involves claiming a promise that God has to honor."

"How so?" asked Meg.

"As I understand it," I explained, "God created the universe by speaking it into existence, and we Christians, being children of God, can command this same power. Thus, if you make a confession by reciting a promise from the scriptures, whatever you ask for comes to fruition. Name it, claim it."

"Dang!" said Noylene, who had finished her bussing, had wandered up and been listening in. "Where in the Bible does it say that?"

"Mark 11:22 and 23. 'I tell you the truth, if anyone says to this mountain, 'Go, throw yourself into the sea,' and does not doubt in his heart but believes that what he says will happen, it will be done for him.' And hence, Brother Hog can't argue he didn't cause the fire without going against his own beliefs. I'm pretty sure he isn't going to do that."

"Then it *is* his fault," said Nancy.

"Probably not," said Pete. "But he can't say that it's not. If he does, he's finished at New Fellowship."

"Yep," I said. "Right now, he's riding high. Of course, if the church is found liable, his stock is likely to go down considerably."

"Why would the church be liable?" asked Dave, who'd joined us as well.

"Russ Stafford's position is that Brother Hog was acting as the church's agent," said Pete. "One thing's for sure. Those Baptists are getting pretty steamed at ol' Russ. Why don't you ask them about it? I saw a couple of the elders working at the Bible Bazaar."

"I think I will," I said.

Nancy looked over at me. "Hey, I just thought of something. You and Meg are probably going to be called as witnesses. You were the only ones there who weren't part of the protest."

"Yeah," I said.

"We've already gotten our subpoenas," Meg added glumly.

The cowbell on the door jangled, and two men in their mid-twenties came in, looking around like they needed some help or at least some information. They spotted Nancy's uniform and walked over to the table. They both were sporting the requisite three-day beard stubble, LL Bean pre-faded polo shirts, mock-baseball caps, distressed jeans and expensive hiking boots. Designer sunglasses hung around each of their necks on leather lanyards.

"Hi, there," said the taller of the two. "We're looking for the place where the diamonds were discovered."

"You're the third group of prospectors today," said Pete. He pointed out the window and across the park at St. Barnabas. "They were found right over there, under the church, about a hundred years ago."

"No," said the other man. "The diamonds that were found in the cave. You know, it was in all the papers."

"Ah," I said. "Also a hundred years ago. Sorry boys, but that land is privately owned. All the mineral rights are held by one person." I looked over at Noylene. She just smiled and kept clearing one of the dirty tables.

"The paper made it sound like the cave was in a national forest," said the first.

"Well, it might be," I said. "Nobody's ever found the cave. Pisgah National Forest is huge—over half a million acres from south of Asheville all the way to Virginia. There are a couple of big wilderness areas, but most of it's privately owned. The particular property mentioned in the AP report is one of those."

"Quail Ridge?" said the first man.

"Yep," I said. "Private property."

"So, even if we found the cave?" asked the second.

"Anything on that property belongs to the owner," I said. "And last I heard, she wasn't in the mood for claim-jumpers."

"Oh, well," said the first with a shrug. "At least it's a good day for a hike. How 'bout some breakfast?"

"Grab a seat," said Pete. "Noylene will be right over to take your order."

•••

The theological discussion had ebbed, and we were all heading back to our respective morning activities. I was standing outside the Slab on the sidewalk, surveying the square and counting my blessings that we'd decided not to give out any parking tickets to out-of-towners. Noylene suddenly appeared at my side, wiping her hands on her apron and looking distraught.

"Can I talk to you for a minute?" she asked. "I have a problem."

"Sure. What's up?"

"Russ Stafford has been after me since Christmas to sell him the back forty on Quail Ridge. I think he wants to do some sort of deal up there.

"Wormy said something about it. He said you weren't interested in selling."

"I'm not," said Noylene. "But since Sunday, he's really been putting the pressure on. I've got about a hundred and thirty acres up there. Been in the family since the 1940s. My trailer sits right in the front of the property. It was the only way I could get electric."

"Okay," I said. "So what's the problem?"

"Here's the thing. Russ has a camp up on the backside of the ridge. It's been there for years. He wheeled an old camper in, and him and his buddies use it when they go hunting."

"Yeah?"

"Now I get this certified letter. It came this morning." She handed it to me.

I read it quickly. Russ Stafford was suing Noylene for quiet title of most of Quail Ridge under the adverse possession statute. A hundred and ten acres worth.

"Oh, man!" I said.

Noylene went pale. "You mean he can jes' take it!?

"Did you ever give Russ permission to use the property?" I asked.

Noylene shook her head. "Not once! Thought I was being nice, so I never said anything. I wasn't usin' it for nothin'.."

"It says here that Russ has been using the property exclusively for twenty-one years."

"That'd be about right," said Noylene.

"How about improvements? Russ make any improvements?"

"He did some clearing, pulled some dead stumps out. He made a pasture on the backside and planted corn for the deer. Cut down a few dead trees. I never said anything. I figured he was doing it out of kindness 'cause I let him hunt on it. Then Wormy told me yesterday, he's built him a little cabin back there."

"You didn't ever use the property? Farm some of it maybe? Graze some cows?"

Noylene set her mouth hard and shook her head again. "It's about those diamonds, ain't it?"

"I suspect so."

"Is this legal?" she asked in flat voice.

"I'm afraid it is," I said, handing the letter back to her. "You might take him to court for a while. Hold him up. But he has enough here to make it stick. Maybe you should go ahead and sell it to him if he'll still buy it."

"In a pig's eye," snarled Noylene.

•••

The last afternoon of Bible Bazaar 31 A.D. promised to be memorable. To begin with, all the children were finishing up their various projects and making ready for the concluding ceremony, which would take place inside the temple tent and would include the presentation of certificates to all participating children; a brief presentation by Cynthia and her disciples of belly-dancing, all decked out in the beads, veils and other accessories they'd fashioned in the jewelry shop; some Hebrew prayers (recited in unison) that the children had learned; a few songs sung; and most of the crafts laid out on colorful blankets for the kids' parents to "Ooo" and "Ah" over and then take home.

The memorial garden was abuzz. Kimberly Walnut had informed everyone who would listen that the skit would be at 4:45, to give everyone enough time to prepare for the other activities. It was at about 4:30 that people started noticing a distinct lack of children. The tent-mothers were in their usual places, chatting around the well and having their afternoon tea at the herbalist's. The shopkeepers were a lot less busy than usual. Seymour Krebbs didn't have much of a line at the camel ride. I decided that it was time for me to do a little tax-collecting. I'd been pretty lax on the first couple of days. It was time for these kids to render unto Caesar.

I caught the first remnant cowering behind the tent of the tribe of Naphtali. He'd seen me coming and darted into the tent, but I suspected he'd duck under the canvas and try to hide in the back. Sure enough, I found him cowering behind a black chokeberry bush.

"I've come to collect the Roman tax, " I growled, extending a hand. I didn't know him—one of the kids from the Methodist or Baptist congregations. A slight boy, maybe six years old.

"Please, sir," he whimpered. "I don't have any more coins."

"Didn't your tent-mother just give you some?" I asked, surprised.

"Yes, sir." He was on the verge of tears.

"Did you spend them already?"

"No, sir."

"What happened to them?" I asked.

"I can't tell you," he said. "They'll kill me."

I laughed and squatted down beside him, no mean feat in a tunic that was a bit too short for comfort.

"What's your name?" I asked.

"Kevin."

"They won't kill you, Kevin. C'mon. Tell me what's going on and we'll go sort it out."

The boy looked relieved. "It's those 'Piscopals. They took everyone hostage."

•••

It seems that while the tent-mothers were having their tea and Kimberly Walnut was worrying about the skit and the shopkeepers were putting all the crafts in order, the tribe of Issachar had taken over much of the camp, one tent at a time, with a stealth that had to be admired. The Naphtali tent was empty, but Kevin pointed silently to the next tent over. Benjamin. The flaps were closed and when I pulled them apart and stepped inside, I found ten scared children sitting in the corner of the tent, their hands bound behind them with leather thongs and Dewey standing guard over them, a spear in one hand and a sword in the other. He was wearing a leather breastplate over his tunic and a matching headband. Wrist bands and flip-flops completed the outfit.

"Dewey," I growled. "Come with me."

Dewey's eyes went wide and he followed me meekly out of the tent.

"Kevin," I said, "go inside and untie them. If you need help, go get your tent-mother."

77

Kevin darted inside the tent, and I put an ominous hand on Dewey's shoulder. "Which tent is next?" I asked.

Dewey pointed to the tent with the Zebulun sign in front. "We only used the ones that had flaps," he said. "That way, we wouldn't be discovered until our mission was accomplished."

I walked him over to the Zebulun tent. "And what was your mission?"

"To get all the coins, of course. That was my idea," he said proudly. "Samantha planned it. She's great!"

"Then what?"

"Then we take the coins to the candy shop, buy all the candy, and disappear."

I opened the flaps, walked in and found the same situation that I'd found in the previous tent. This time it was Bernadette standing guard and twelve little frightened faces looking back at me. Bernadette looked like a Celtic warrior queen. Boudica, maybe. Her hair was wild and she was adorned with some sort of green face paint. She was leveling a spear at the nearest prisoner. Her face fell when she saw me come in. I took the spear out of her hand and snapped it in half.

"The jig is up," I said.

Kevin came running in a moment later. "The rest of them are in Asher," he said.

I left Kevin to free the prisoners and took Bernadette and Dewey with me to the next tent. I pushed them in ahead of me and followed a moment later. Moosey and Samantha were sitting on the ground dividing a huge mound of candy into six smaller piles. Christopher was standing guard over about fifteen kids, not tied like the others, but all sitting quietly at the back of the tent. Christopher had a sword in one hand and a dagger in the other and would occasionally jab one of them toward a hostage in a threatening manner. Ashley was busy tying their ex-friend Robert to a tree stump that the Asher tent-mother had been using as a table. I was afraid to ask the reason. Some sort of sacrifice, I presumed.

"Oh, crap," said Samantha, when she saw me.

"Oh, crap, indeed," I replied. "The law is here. Let's go."

The six of them piled their weapons on the ground and lined up. "What about the candy?" asked Moosey.

"Spoils of war, I think they call it," I said. "Anyway, that's the least of your problems. Your tent-mother is going to open up a can of whupass on you guys."

"You can't say 'whupass' to us," said Ashley. "We're just little kids."

•••

I wasn't far off. Meg was so mad I thought we might have another Slaughter of the Innocents on our hands. Cooler heads prevailed, though, and after an *almost* sincere apology from the tribe of Issachar to the rest of Israel, all seemed to be forgiven, especially since the other eleven tribes were allowed to split all the ill-gotten candy. By the time everything had been sorted out, it was a little past five o'clock.

Kimberly Walnut was in a tither. She might have gotten over the fact that six of the ten-year-old Bible-Schoolers had managed to forge their own weapons, take most of the camp hostage while the mothers were drinking tea, steal everyone's coins, and almost make off with all the candy. Yes, she might have gotten past all of it, except that now *her schedule was off!* She ran back and forth like a rabid sheepdog, herding each group over to the drama area where they dutifully plopped onto the ground for another episode of "The New Testament According to Kimberly Walnut." This episode was entitled *The Stoning of Stephen.*

The tent-mothers were standing in the back, all of them keeping a close eye on the Issachar gang. Cynthia stood near me, looking mighty fine in her belly-dancing outfit, and chatting with Noylene who had wandered over from the Beautifery.

"Look at this," Noylene was saying, holding her hands in front of her face and blowing on her nails. "It's called *Passionella Pink.* Brand new. It's gonna be a bestseller."

"Lovely," said Cynthia, catching my eye and making a wry face.

Father Tony was decked out in his high priest togs. Ardine, Bud and Pauli Girl had come to pick up Moosey and were standing next to Father Tony. The two Roman soldiers were lurking at the edges, as Roman soldiers do, and the shopkeepers had arrived on the scene as well. The beggar and the leper were still working the crowd. Apparently no one had informed them that all the coins were gone. Even Seymour Krebbs had abandoned his camel for a moment to watch the festivities.

Kimberly Walnut was the narrator for this skit, and quite a skit it was.

"Stephen was full of grace and power," she said, doing a pretty good impression of Charlton Heston. "And he did great wonders among the people."

St. Stephen, played by Russ Stafford, took center stage and did his best to look like he was full of power and grace. It was a stretch.

Varmit Lemieux stepped forward, a plant from the audience. "We have heard him speak against God!" he said. "This man is always speaking against the holy Temple and against the law of Moses. We have heard him say that this Jesus will destroy the Temple and change the customs Moses handed down to us."

Father Tony piped up as well, in his role as high priest. "Is this true?" he intoned.

Russ began his sermon. "You stubborn people! You are deaf to the truth. Must you forever resist the Holy Spirit? That's what your ancestors did, and so do you! Name one prophet your ancestors didn't persecute! They even killed the ones who predicted the coming of the Jesus whom you betrayed and murdered. You deliberately disobeyed God's law."

It was at this point that several large baskets started being passed through the crowd—baskets containing large, gray styrofoam rocks about the size of grapefruits.

"The Jews were furious with Stephen," thundered Kimberly, "and they shook their fists with rage."

She shook her fist at Russ and hissed at him. The kids caught on quickly and soon everyone in the crowd was shaking their fists and booing him. Russ looked especially serene.

"Look," he hollered above the din, pointing at the sky.

"I see the heavens opened and the Son of Man standing in the place of honor at God's right hand!"

Kimberly Walnut threw the first styrofoam rock. It bounced off Russ' shoulder. It was followed by a slew of rocks, most of which didn't make it to the stage due to the relative weight of styrofoam, wind resistance, and eight-year-old throwing arms. Many of the projectiles landed in the crowd and bounced harmlessly off uncounted heads with more than a few giggles. This didn't stop Russ from falling to his knees and crying, "Lord Jesus, receive my spirit, and don't charge them with this sin!"

The kids, most of whose rocks had fallen short, came forward in a surge, picked up the light-weight boulders and, laughing, made sure they were near enough to pummel Russ from close range. Some adults moved toward Russ as well, tossing the odd piece of styrofoam toward the pile of children, and generally getting into the spirit of the play. It was a mass of people, young and old, all laughing and having a jolly time. Much, I thought ironically, like it might have been at a *real* stoning.

After a few minutes, the adults started collecting the kids and moving them over to the temple tent for the final ceremony. It was quite a mob scene, good enough to work in any Monty Python movie. I smiled, shook my head, then turned and walked to the tent with the rest of them.

We stood through Father Tony's opening prayer, Kimberly Walnut's thank-yous, the prize for the best tent, and the conferring of the certificates. Cynthia and the little belly-dancers had just begun their routine when I felt a hand on my arm. I turned and saw Gerry Flemming. He was white as a ghost.

"You'd better come quick," he whispered. "Russ is dead."

Chapter 9

Choir practice was called off, of course. We spent the three hours securing the scene of Mr. Stafford's untimely demise, first getting the children out of the park—not a difficult task, since their parents were picking them up, anyway—then making sure that Brianna was taken care of, and finally calling the ambulance to take his body down to the morgue for an autopsy. I didn't think we needed one. It was pretty clear how Russ met his fate, but it was protocol in a murder investigation. We went over the crime scene several times, Dave taking pictures, and Nancy taking notes. Russ Stafford's body had been lying just where we'd left him when the play concluded, stretched out amidst a good-sized pile of styrofoam boulders and one large, melon-sized piece of granite that seemed to fit perfectly into the indentation in Russ' head. The stone matched the granite that had been used for the exterior of the new church, a left-over piece dropped under a bush or kicked behind a tree. Nancy took the murder weapon over to the police station and locked it up. Tomorrow it would go to the lab in Boone for DNA analysis and fingerprinting. After we'd finished, Nancy and Dave came up to the house at my invitation. Supper was at Meg's insistence.

The three of us were sitting at the kitchen table, drinking beer and anticipating the shrimp pasta that Meg was putting together at the sink. Baxter was being scratched behind the ears by Nancy and, judging from the way his tail was thumping a back beat on the kitchen floor, had found true love.

"This is great," Dave said, taking a sip and looking at the bottle. "Sprecher Black Bavarian Style Lager. Where do you get this stuff?"

"I have my sources," I said smugly.

"Beer of the Month Club," said Meg, putting the bowl of pasta in the center of the table. "Help yourselves. The bread's coming out of the oven in a minute."

We followed Meg's directive and, in a moment, the four of us were digging into a delicious meal.

"Did you get Skeeter out of the clink?" I asked Nancy.

She shook her head. "Forgot all about it. I'll go down there tomorrow morning. It won't hurt him to stay there for another night."

"I don't suppose it was an accident?" said Meg. "Russ, I mean."

"Nope," said Dave. "That rock probably weighed twenty pounds. Hard to mistake it for styrofoam."

"Well," said Meg, "then I suppose the question is, who hated Russ enough to kill him?"

"It's not always about hate," I said. "Sometimes it's about expedience."

"Or justice," said Nancy. "Or revenge."

"Jealousy," added Dave. "Greed."

I nodded. "So the question we need to ask is not who hated Russ enough to kill him, but rather, who wanted Russ dead? Pass me a piece of that bread, will you?"

"Hmm," said Meg, passing me the plate of bread. "Okay. Who wanted Russ dead?"

"Any number of people," I said. "Russ was a singularly dislikable man with very little moral character."

Meg looked at me expectantly.

"Okay," I said. "Let's go through the list. Just the people who were at the Bible Bazaar. It had to be one of them."

Nancy pulled out her pad and pen.

"Hmm," I said. "I suppose we can put one of those Fellowship Baptist elders on the list. With Russ dead, I'm guessing that lawsuit will go away and Francis Passaglio will take the insurance settlement. Since the referendum didn't pass, Brother Hog remains a hero and the church isn't out the two million dollars."

"Two million dollars?" said Meg. "That old feed store wasn't worth two million dollars!"

"That's what he was suing for. Actual damages, loss of income, and damage to the establishment's reputation."

"Still...murder?" asked Meg.

"Sure," said Nancy. "How about Noylene?" I had filled Nancy in on Noylene's plight earlier in the afternoon.

"How *about* Noylene?" asked Meg, obviously shocked.

"Russ was getting ready to take her property—most of Quail Ridge, actually—under a little-used statute called Adverse Possession. I'm pretty sure he was planning on doing some diamond mining."

Meg sat there, stunned. "Noylene would never..."

"Sure she would," said Dave. "Noylene's a mountain girl. She wouldn't think twice about protecting what was hers, especially if it had been in her family for years."

"Will Brianna continue with the action?" asked Nancy. "This pasta's great, by the way." Meg smiled her thanks.

"Nope," I said, shaking my head. "She can't. Russ was the only one who could have filed the suit because he was the only one who used the property."

"So with Russ dead...?" said Dave.

"The point is moot," I said. "Noylene keeps her property. And you can bet she won't make the same mistake again. How about another beer?"

"I'll take one," said Nancy.

"I'm the one driving," said Dave. "Thanks, though."

Meg shook her head, then said, "Is that everyone?"

"Ardine McCollough," I said, getting up and getting two more brews out of the fridge. "Pauli Girl. Maybe Bud."

"*What?*" said Dave and Nancy at the same time.

I looked over at Meg. She sighed.

"We think that Pauli Girl's been molested," she said. "Or at least someone tried. I don't know for sure because she wouldn't tell me. Ardine certainly thought so."

"Russ?" asked Nancy.

"We all think it was someone connected to the youth group at the church. An adult. That would be either Russ or Gerry Flemming."

"Or Brianna," said Dave, with a wink. "Or maybe Wilma."

"Hadn't thought of that," Meg said. "But you're right."

"I think we can assume it was Russ," I said. "Since he's the one who's dead."

"But what if it *was* Ardine that killed him and she made a mistake?" Meg said.

"Good point. Ardine's certainly no shrinking violet, and we all know that she's settled some scores in the past, but we also can't discount Pauli Girl, if indeed, she was molested. She was standing right there, and she might have taken the opportunity to even things up."

"What about Bud?" said Dave.

"Ardine was talking with him the day before. It's why he missed his entrance during the skit. I wonder what his mother said to him."

"You think he was protecting his sister?" said Nancy.

I shrugged. "Can't discount it."

"How about Brianna?" said Meg.

We all looked at her, blankly, waiting for an explanation.

"She's Russ' wife, for heaven's sake! Maybe she found out that he'd molested Pauli Girl." Meg narrowed her gaze. "Maybe Pauli Girl wasn't the first."

"Holy smokes!" said Dave. "Never thought of that."

"Anyone else?" I asked.

"Anyone left?" said Nancy.

Chapter 10

Dr. Kent Murphee was a curmudgeon, easily identifiable by his tweed suit. Only a curmudgeon wears a tweed suit in June. Lovable, yes, but a curmudgeon nevertheless.

"I hate to get up early on a Friday," he grumbled, busily tamping down the tobacco in his pipe with the end of his fountain pen.

"It's ten o'clock," I said. "And it's Thursday."

"Ten o'clock, you say. How about a drink then?" he asked, pulling open his right-hand desk drawer and coming up with a bottle of bourbon.

"I dunno, Kent," I said. "If I start drinking at ten o'clock now, I won't have anything to look forward to when I'm your age."

Kent, the Watauga County coroner, was in his late fifties, but looked ten years older, partly due to genetics, partly due to a little too much to drink. His office was located in Boone. We didn't have a coroner in St. Germaine. We didn't have a hospital. We didn't even have a full-time doctor.

"Yeah, yeah," he groused, pushing a glass across the desk in my direction. "If you want some ice, there's some in that box over there." He waved a finger toward a white plastic chest in the corner.

"Kent," I said, not unkindly, "isn't that what they use to transport organs for transplant?"

"Yeah," said Kent. "But the dry ice is great in a drink. Just use the tongs. You don't want to get that stuff on your hands."

"I'll just have mine straight," I said. "Now, how about that body we sent down yesterday?"

Kent looked across the desk at me and stroked his chin. "You know there's a national park in Canada where the Indians used to run buffalo over a cliff?"

I shrugged and gave him a puzzled look.

"It's called 'Head-Bashed-In-Buffalo-Jump.' I visited there last summer. You know what they say when you call for information?"

I shrugged again, this time smiling.

"Head-Bashed-In. May I help you?"

That brought a laugh.

"So, you're saying..."

"Head bashed in."

I chuckled. "Anything in the wound?"

"Not much. He had a lot of hair, though. I'll say that for him."

"He was a real estate salesman. Used cars, too."

"Ah," said Kent, with a knowing look. "That explains it. Anyway, some dirt, other debris. Did you find the weapon?"

"A big rock. It's down at the lab."

"Sounds about right. I can match it exactly if you need me to. There's a pretty nice impression on the victim's skull."

I finished my drink, stood up, and reached across the desk to shake Kent's hand. "I'll let you know," I said. "Probably won't need to if the blood and the tissue match, but I'll keep you in the loop."

"Always glad to help," said Kent.

•••

"We have two problems," said Bev Greene.

"We have more than *that!*" said Kimberly Walnut.

"Number one," said Bev, ignoring her. "Now that the building is finished, we've got to find a full-time rector. Father Tony will only stay until the end of the summer. The last Sunday in August, he says goodbye for good. That gives us less than three months."

I generally avoided church staff meetings as a rule. Thursday afternoons weren't especially busy, but even so, the criminal element in St. Germaine certainly didn't take Thursday afternoons off. That was my argument anyway. I suspected that, in reality, it *did* take Thursday afternoons off. Now, I was just hoping for some gunplay down at Noylene's Beautifery to shake me loose—something that had been known to happen on occasion, especially when one of the new girls mixed up "Blue Rinse" with "Blue Wench," apparently two distinctly different hair products.

"How about getting a headhunter?" I said.

"What's that?" asked Marilyn. Besides Marilyn, the long-suffering secretary of St. Barnabas and the only one who truly knew what was going on, the meeting included Bev, Kimberly, Joyce Cooper, who had been in charge of the welcoming ministry for more than a few years, Georgia, and myself. Father Tony was always invited, of course, but hadn't made a meeting yet.

"You know, a headhunter," I said again. "Someone to go out and find who we want, offer him or her a much better salary than he's currently making, and spirit him into St. Germaine in the dead of night."

"Do you think that would work?"

I shrugged. "Maybe. Might be worth a try."

"I'll run it past the vestry," said Bev, jotting notes to herself. "I wonder if it's at all ethical."

"I guess we could always ask the bishop for help," said Joyce. That brought a laugh from everyone.

"Ethical, schmethical," said Georgia. "We need a priest!"

"Number two," said Bev. "Diamonds." She threw up her hands. "Now we're sitting on diamonds. What are we going to do about *that*?"

"I've been thinking about it," said Joyce. "and I suggest we draw up an amendment to our charter forbidding any digging for diamonds on church property."

"Can we do that?" asked Bev, looking at me.

I thought for a moment. "It's the right idea, but it would be easier just to restrict all the mineral rights to the property. Maybe put them in an irrevocable trust for, say, a hundred years."

"I'll ask the lawyers about it," said Bev, making another note.

"Now, what about those kids?" Kimberly demanded, the ball finally falling into her court.

"What kids are those, dear?" said Bev, sweetly.

"Those little terrorists who tried to hijack my Bible Bazaar!"

"Oh, they're fine," said Joyce, with a laugh. "Kids will be kids, after all. The important thing is to keep them busy."

"I agree," said Georgia. "As long as they have something to do here at the church, it's far less likely that we'll have another incident like last summer."

Bev and Joyce nodded gravely.

"What happened last summer?" asked Kimberly suspiciously.

"Best you don't know," said Bev. "We've all tried very hard to put it behind us."

•••

It was June, but cool enough to have a fire going in the fireplace and, if there *was* a fire (and there was), Baxter would be lying in front of it on his old rug. Meg was curled up on the couch. Archimedes was preening himself atop the head of my stuffed buffalo, a present from Meg some years back that she had procured from some Western-style eatery going out of business. I was feeling pretty smug about the whole set-up.

"Maybe you could start a children's choir," suggested Meg. She'd finished her biography and was now reading *The Shack*.

"Maybe not," I said, feeling a cold chill creep up my neck. I flipped on the light over my typewriter and stuck Raymond Chandler's fedora firmly on my head.

"I think you should read this book when I'm finished with it. You'd like it."

"Doesn't matter if I'd like it or not," I said. "I won't read it. It's too popular. Maybe in a few years." I rolled a new sheet of paper into the old machine.

"You are so odd," said Meg, looking at me with a smile. "What's on the stereo? I really like it. It's beautiful."

"That's the soundtrack from the film *A River Runs Through It*."

"That's why I like it. I *loved* that movie. You know," she said, "maybe all the good composers have turned to film. That's why I can't listen to the academics."

"No doubt about it," I said.

"Who's the composer?"

"Fellow named Mark Isham."

•••

Wiggy went by the title of "pastor," though his ordination was obtained on the World-Wide Interweb for the cost of five dollars. Pastor Wiggy Newland. It had a ring to it, the kind of ring that cash registers made when old ladies sent in their Social Security checks to Pastor Wiggy's tax-exempt address in Weehauken, Wisconsin. Of course, Wiggy would no longer be going by the title of "pastor." Now he had a new name. Mort.

•••

I read over the page and smiled to myself. No doubt about it. The hat and the typewriter were working their magic.

"Erich Korngold was the first classical guy to make a big name for himself as a film composer," I said. "*Captain Blood, Sea Wolf, The Adventures of Robin Hood* and a lot of others."

"Hmm," said Meg, changing the subject. "You know, if you started a children's choir, it would give those kids an appreciation of music that would last the rest of their lives."

"Not a chance," I said. "Who put you up to this?"

Meg suddenly looked very guilty. "Well...someone brought it up at the vestry meeting. I'm not saying who."

"Bev? Elaine? Kimberly Walnut?"

"I told you, I'm not saying."

"It was *you*, wasn't it?"

"Look," said Meg. "It would be a good thing. Just for the summer. Then you can quit."

"Nope." I looked back at my typewriter, knowing that I was doomed.

"I'll make it worth your while," Meg said.

"Oh, man!" I whined.

Meg walked up behind me and whispered something delicious in my ear.

"Okay, *fine!*" I grumbled, half-heartedly. "But I'm picking the music."

•••

I needed to talk to Pedro. He was right where I thought he'd be, decorating our regular table at Buxtehooters with cigar butts and empty shot glasses. Pedro LaFleur was my right-hand man, big as a really big bear and cranky as a ten-pound baby with a twelve-pound diaper. He sang counter-tenor for the Presbyterians in his spare time or whenever Orlando Gibbons showed up in the anthem rotation, but mostly he was a heck of a gumshoe. He also drank like a fish, the kind of fish that consumes huge quantities of scotch and passes out on the beach.

"Did you know the dead guy?" I asked. "Wiggy Newland?"

"No, but I did some checking," said Pedro. "According to my snitch, he's been in dutch ever since he was belched out of his mother's angry, belligerent womb. He was sent to baby-juvie when he was three, regular-juvie when he was eight, and didn't come out until he was pardoned by the archbishop for arranging to sell indulgences to Southern Baptists who thought they were buying Get-Out-Of-Hell-Free cards. After that, he went full-time into the ministry scam."

"Anything else?"

Pedro sat back in his chair.

"He's been dealing diamonds."

"You know where he was getting them?"

"I know where. Just not how. I do know that Picket the Fence was funding his retirement plan. There's also a skirt involved."

"Constance Noring?"

"That's the one. They'd been making Bible-study trips to Australia every three months."

"They take a missionary position?"

Pedro snorted. "Not if I know Constance."

I nodded knowingly.

"I doubt that the diamond mines of Humptydoo are the new mission fields," he continued. "They're smugglers."

"So the church gig was a front."

"It brought in a pretty penny, no doubt," said Pedro, "but it was a laundering operation."

Pedro was seldom wrong. He had a sense about these things, like someone who can tell butter from I Can't Believe It's Not Butter.

"You know where the money was going?"

"Workin' on it. Why don't you give Twelve-Fingered Teddy a rattle? He might know something."

"I'll do that."

Chapter 11

"Okay, it's been a week. What have we got?" I asked, as I banged into the police station.

"We've got donuts," offered Dave.

"We've got some leftover coffee from yesterday," said Nancy. "Other than that, we've got zilch."

Nancy's motorcycle helmet was resting on the counter, holding down a stack of papers. Nancy was a motorcycle cop in the summer, having outfitted her Harley with a couple of blinking blue lights. In the winter, she tooled around in her old Nissan sedan and longed for summer. She moved her helmet and rifled through the papers.

"Nothing from the lab. No fingerprints on the rock, and the only DNA samples they could get were from the victim. Blood, hair and a little bit of tissue. All from Russ Stafford. The rock weighed in at thirty-four pounds."

"We've got our work cut out for us," I said.

Nancy and Dave both nodded. Dave offered me the box of donuts.

"Sorry, Chief," said Dave. "I ate all the jelly ones."

I made the kind of executive decision for which I was famous and went with powdered sugar. "So," I said, "what we need is a confession."

"That'd be good," said Nancy. "Shall I get the rubber hoses?"

"Not yet," I said with a smile. "We need to know who we're dealing with first. Go and get the names of the adults who were there from New Fellowship Baptist."

"We're presuming that it wasn't a kid who killed him?" asked Dave.

"For now," I said. "I'm thinking a kid would have left a print or some DNA or something. This was planned."

"Okay," said Nancy. "That Walnut woman gave me a list of everyone who was signed up to work. I'll narrow it down to the adults from the Baptist church."

"It's a start," I said. "We'll look for motive and work backwards. How many people knew that the last skit was *The Stoning of Stephen?*"

"Everyone," said Nancy. "The schedule was posted in everyone's tent and on the bulletin board they set up beside the drama area."

I walked around the counter and back to my cluttered office, dropped into my chair behind the desk, and pushed some paperwork off to the side. Most of our paperwork concerned filling out state forms. Whatever Dave couldn't manage, he'd leave on my desk. I'd get to it.

"Let's have a list," I called.

Nancy and Dave both appeared at the door.

"Other than the Baptists?" Nancy asked.

"Yeah."

She pulled out her pad and read.

"Ardine, Bud and Pauli Girl McCollough, Noylene Fabergé-Dupont, Hogmanay McTavish—aka Brother Hog—and maybe Brianna Stafford."

"Scratch Brother Hog," I said. "He wasn't there, and he's so fat someone would have recognized him."

Nancy put a line through his name.

"How about Ardine?"

"I don't think so," I said. "Not her style. She's more of a poisoner."

In addition to her ex-husband PeeDee, a nasty, abusive piece of work who had mysteriously gone missing many years ago, Ardine had been involved in another case, the murder of one Willie Boyd. Mr. Boyd had been dispatched by one of the oldest and revered techniques in the hills for ending an unhappy marriage: oleander poisoning. Before divorces became easily obtained, it was very difficult for a woman in these hills to rid herself of an abusive or unfaithful husband, and a cup of oleander tea solved the problem. The heart attack that followed was rarely diagnosed, since life expectancy up here in the hills wasn't that great to begin with. After the law changed and a woman could file for divorce herself, the mortality rate of married males, aged twenty to fifty, went down sixty percent. Mr. Boyd wasn't married to Ardine, but he was pretending that he was and blackmailing her for favors unbecoming a lady. I couldn't prove any of this, of course, so it was all just conjecture on my part. Ardine hadn't denied it, but she hadn't admitted to it, either. No charges were ever filed.

"She *could* have done it," Nancy said. She and Dave knew all about Willie Boyd.

"Yeah, she could have," I agreed. "I'll go talk to her. Pauli Girl, too."

"Okay," said Nancy. "I'll put together that list."

•••

St. Germaine was in full bloom. I walked out of the police station and looked across Sterling Park, thought about cutting across, but decided to meander around the square and do my police-chief-checking-on-the-town thing à la Andy Griffith. St. Germaine had a lot going for it these days; principally, a lovely downtown, thanks to a mayor who, in 1961, made it a crime to cut down any healthy mature tree in the historic district under penalty of a $1000 fine—quite a bit of money back then. The result of this ordinance was that, since new construction generally required clearing some land, most business owners chose to remain downtown in their old buildings and refurbish them rather than move to a newer and less picturesque site. There were a few businesses that bucked this trend, the Piggly Wiggly Grocery Store, for example, but they had to pay the City Council a pretty penny for the privilege. The likeness of this "man of foresight and wisdom," as the plaque read, now stood in the center of the park named after him—Harrison Sterling.

Most of the stores and offices located on the square were decorated with flower boxes or planters containing every blossom from ageratums to zinnias. My old Chevy truck was parked in front of the station, and, as I walked by, I opened the driver's side door and rooted around under the seat until I found my cell phone. It was dead, of course, having been under the seat for the better part of a week, but I had promised Meg I'd find it and do my level best to hang onto it. During the winter, my phone worked just fine, and I carried it all the time. The problem was that as soon as all the leaves came out, my phone only worked sporadically, and even then it seemed as if I had to be standing on one foot in the middle of the park to get any reception. The mice living under the seat of my truck hadn't chewed it up too badly, at least as far as I could tell.

The square was bustling. I walked down the sidewalk, greeting visitors and residents alike, and turned left at the corner. I waved through the window of Eden Books at Georgia, who was busily checking customers out behind the register, then continued on my trek. I passed Noylene's Beautifery (closed until eleven) and saw Wormy getting out of his truck by the side dumpster.

"Morning, Wormy!" I called. "Care to join me for a cup of joe?"

"No, thanks," he called back with a grin. "I gotta get back to work.

94

I think I've got the whereabouts of that cave narrowed down."

He lifted an old box out of the back of his pick-up and tossed it into the dumpster.

"Noylene says I can't throw this stuff down the mountain anymore," he said, a little disgust evident in his voice. "She says I have to bring it all into town. I offered to burn it, but she said no."

"Probably for the best," I agreed.

"Bah," said Wormy. "It's only rags and stuff left over from that Bible show."

"Look on the bright side, Wormy," I said. "Now you're an environmentalist. You can put that on your business cards for Wormy Acres."

He bucked up immediately. "Yeah! Hey, yeah! That's a great idea! I'll go tell Noylene!"

I crossed North Main Street and stopped in at The Ginger Cat a couple of doors down. Annie Cooke, the owner, was behind the counter. Her establishment was full of shoppers, happy to take a break from their labors with a cup of tea, a scone and some homemade preserves.

"Morning, Annie," I said.

"Morning. What can I get you?"

"Large coffee to go."

"How about some Mexican Altura Coatepec?"

"If that's coffee, I'll take it."

The Ginger Cat was an upscale yuppie eatery and coffee house that offered sandwiches on fancy foreign breads, generally unpronounceable coffees, and knickknacks by mountain artisans. They also had a selection of local wines for which Bud had written enticing reviews. I put my three dollars on the counter, bid Annie adieu, took my cup, and walked back out into the morning.

The Bear and Brew was going back up. Francis had settled with the insurance company almost immediately upon Russ' demise and started rebuilding. I thought for a moment about Francis and discarded his motive almost immediately. If the church had *lost* the suit that Russ had filed, New Fellowship Baptist would have had to cough up much more than the insurance company would have to pay out. Added to that, Brianna Stafford still owned sixty percent of the business. If the church had *won* the lawsuit, the insurance company still would have paid. It was win-win for the Bear and

Brew. No reason that I could see for the junior partner to kill the senior partner.

I took a sip of coffee, headed toward the next corner, turned left again and followed the sidewalk toward St. Barnabas. I thought about anyone else who might have had a motive to kill Russ Stafford, but came up empty. I passed the gazebo in Sterling Park, a white, Victorian-looking structure left over from when St. Germaine had a community band that played concerts once a month during the summer. There was always talk of bringing the concerts back, a return to the days of yesteryear, but it hadn't happened yet. I waved at some kids who were using the gazebo as a base for their game of tag.

Billy was outside the church weed-eating the edge of the sidewalk. He had on a pair of ear-protectors as well as his goggles. I gave him a wave as I walked by, and he returned it with with a smile. Just past the church, I turned left, stopped into the flower shop and ordered a dozen roses for Meg. Red roses.

"Anniversary?" asked Sandy.

"Yep," I said. "Anniversary of the second...no, *third* time I asked Meg to marry me. Of course, she said no."

"Smart girl," said Sandy.

"But then, she eventually said yes," I replied.

"Like I said..." said Sandy with a grin.

•••

I walked into St. Barnabas at 6:30 and heard the unmistakable sounds of Max Reger's *Basso ostinato in E minor* emanating forth from the organ. All week, Michael Baum had been working his artistry, putting his final stamp on the instrument. It sounded to me as if he'd accomplished his objective. The organ case was a work of art in itself, but it was the sound that brought a grin. Magnificent was the only word for it. Michael was a much better organist than I, but if I could make the organ sound half as good as he did, I'd be more than content. I'd probably even find time to practice.

I walked up the steps into the choir loft and took a seat in the alto section, smack-dab in the midst of the sound. Michael gave me a smile and kept playing. Thirty seconds later, he finished with a flourish, and the sound reverberated through the nave just long enough to make me shake my head in appreciation.

"You've had that smile on your face since you walked in," said Michael. "I take it you approve."

"It's brilliant!" I said.

"The voicing is finished," Michael said. "I've checked the midi interface so you can record and play it back. That's all working."

"Great," I said.

"You know there's a handgun in the organ bench?"

"Yeah. That's mine. It's a Glock 9mm. Tends to keep the tenors in tune."

"Ah, of course. Anyway, the zimbelstern is hooked up," he said, pointing at the bells mounted on the upper case. "I also have a surprise for you."

"What's that?"

"Listen." Michael pulled a knob and pushed a key. The sound of birdsong echoed through the church. I was smiling again. It was one of the toy stops that Baroque organs used to have in abundance. This one was comprised of two small organ pipes, mounted upside down and blowing into a water-filled vessel.

"A nachtigal?"

"Yep," said Michael.

"That wasn't in the specs," I said.

"No, but I thought you'd like it."

"I love it!"

"Then my work here is done," said Michael with finality. "I'm just kidding. If you need anything else or if something goes haywire, just give me a call. I think we're fine, but occasionally I miss something."

I nodded, but Michael never missed anything.

•••

The choir wandered in and found their seats to the sounds of Michael Baum's interpretation of Marcello's *Psalm 19*.

"Wow," said Rebecca. "Wish Hayden could play like that."

"Hey," I said. "I'm insulted."

Michael finished to applause, got off the organ bench and took a well-deserved bow.

"It's all yours, now," he said, sitting down and changing his organ shoes for a pair of worn-out Adidas.

"I'll do the best I can," I said.

...

Twelve-Fingered Teddy was a drunk, but that didn't stop him from playing a mean service. Stewed or not, he was the only ivory-jockey in the city who could play the "Polydactic Etudes for Queen Wilhelmina" by Dutch composer Roloff van der Vlees, and he did so with relish --most often sweet pickle, although he occasionally preferred a mild chow-chow if there were frankfurters involved.

"Hello, Teddy," I said when I reached the choir loft. Teddy's eleventh finger slipped off the high G# with a squeal like Al Gore accepting his Nobel Prize.

Teddy unzipped his mouth like a gymbag and sputtered "Whaddyawan?" slurring his crotchets and syllables in equal measure.

"I want some answers. And maybe that hot-dog you've got heating up on the en chamade."

Teddy was a canary with stool pigeon tendencies. If he knew something, you could sprinkle some salt (and by salt, I mean gin) on his tail (and by tail, I mean uvula) and he'd sing like Celine Dion being taunted with a pork-chop. I handed him a flask. He opened it with two fingers while continuing to play the fugue with the other ten.

"So ask," he said, wiping his mouth with one of his feet, the one that wasn't playing a pedal C. "But keep your hands off my wiener."

"You hear anything about any diamonds?"

"Aussi diamonds?"

"Yeah. Aussi diamonds."

"Maybe."

"Listen, Teddy," I said. "Spill your guts, or I'll kick your diapason all the way back to Lizard Lick."

"How did you know?"

"Know what?" I asked.

"How did you know about Lizard Lick?"

"?," I queried.

"The Lizard Lick Creation Museum," said Twelve-Fingered Teddy. "I hear the bishops are fit to be tied."

98

I was speechless. Teddy was positively gluttonous with self-approbation. The hot-dog just sat there, like an inanimate object.

•••

"You know," said Sheila, "this may be the most beautiful thing I've ever read."

All the altos nodded in agreement.

"Thanks," I said. "And just for that, I'm not going to make any altos sing higher than a 'D' this evening."

The altos smiled. "Told you it would work," said Sheila.

"I heard you were starting a children's choir," said Elaine. "What a good idea!"

I couldn't tell exactly if this was sarcasm, but I chose to think better of Elaine. "Just for the summer," I said. "We're meeting on Wednesdays at 5:30; so if you know anyone who's interested, tell them to come."

"Any audition required?" asked Mark.

"Of course," I said.

"No," said Meg. "No audition. Any child who wants to may join."

"Huh?" I said. "Wait a min..."

"It's important that all the children be involved," said Bev. "Whether they're tone-deaf or not."

"*What?* Tone deaf?" I said.

Bev and Meg crossed their arms in a show of solidarity. Elaine chuckled.

"Well, I'm picking the music," I mumbled, holding on to the one shred of control I had left.

"It has to be fun," said Georgia. "Kids won't like it if it's not fun."

"And scriptural," added Muffy Lemieux. "It needs to be the Word of God. Hey! How about a musical?"

"An excellent idea," said Meg happily. "A musical."

"But I'm picking it," I said, my voice getting smaller. "Because I'm the director."

"I saw some kids do a Jonah and the Whale thing over in Johnson City last year," said Steve. "It was a Lutheran Church, I think. I'll bet I could find out the name of it."

99

"You see," I muttered. "I agreed to this because Meg said I would get to choose the music. I was thinking that maybe we'd learn some two-part Heinrich Schütz motets in the original German..."

"Jonah and the Whale would be great!" said Bev. "Or maybe another Bible story. I'm sure that Hayden can find us one."

"This will be fun," said Meg. "I'll help make the costumes."

"Me, too!" said Muffy. "And I can help with make-up."

"We'll build the sets," said Phil. The rest of the men agreed enthusiastically.

"If we can get the music fairly quickly," said Sheila, "rehearsals can start next week. Then the kids could put it on in July."

"Great idea," agreed Bev.

"Because I'm the one in charge," I sighed.

Chapter 12

"I have the list," said Nancy. "I got it from Kimberly Walnut, then confirmed it with Vera Kendrick, the children's minister from New Fellowship Baptist."

"Let's hear it," said Pete.

"Hey," I said. "This is police business."

"Sorry," said Pete.

"So let's hear it," I said.

The Slab Café seemed to stay busy from June straight through to Labor Day. Pete had an "owner's table" by the kitchen, so it was no problem getting a seat, but getting served was another matter entirely. Noylene was busier than a one-armed paper hanger, and Pauli Girl was hustling as well. Cynthia, our mayor, wasn't on the waitress schedule this morning.

"Be with you in a bit," said Noylene as she raced by. "Help yourself to some coffee."

Dave got up and retrieved the coffee pot from the burner. We all held up our empty cups in salute. Dave filled them and then dutifully filled all the cups that the rest of the patrons held aloft as soon as they spied him with a coffee pot.

"Now," I said, once the coffee was poured and Dave had rejoined our table. "Let's hear the list."

"Well," said Nancy, flipping her pad open. "The adults from New Fellowship Baptist who were there for the last bit of *The Stoning of Stephen* skit are as follows. Vera Kendrick. She's the children's minister. The woman working at the basket shop was Jenny Thatcher."

"I don't know her," I said. "You?"

"Nope," said Nancy. "She may not be from St. Germaine. I'll get addresses and phone numbers on all these folks."

I nodded.

"Jenny's husband, Jeremy, was there, too. He was working in the carpenter's tent. They have a six-year-old and an eight-year-old. Both kids were enrolled."

"Okay," I said. "Who else?"

"The girl in the dye shop, the one that said 'Lydia' on the outside, is named Diana Terry. She's a retired teacher."

"Ah, I didn't recognize her," I said. "I know Diana. I don't think she's a suspect."

"Why not?" asked Dave.

"She's an ex-nun," I said. "Call it a hunch."

"The two soldiers are named John Perdue and Jimmy Tinsdale. College students, home for the summer. They're both on the NFB praise team. The man playing the beggar was Mitch St. Claire. Mitch was the only one of the bunch who was at the Bear and Brew the morning it burned down. The weekend before that, he was arrested in Greenville, South Carolina, at a men's Bible conference called *Jesus 2.0—Retool and Reload.* He punched out one of the presenters."

"A fight?"

"More like a mugging. The pastor pressed charges. Mitch St. Claire was arrested and spent the night in lock-up."

"Hmm. Interesting."

"The two college kids didn't even get home till the Saturday before the Bible Bazaar. They weren't in town for Brother Hog's protest."

"Let's talk to them, anyway," I said. "The Thatchers, too. But Brother Mitch sounds like he might be bearing the brunt of our perlustration."

"Huh?" said Dave.

"Bring him in," I said.

•••

Father Tony was walking his beagle in Sterling Park when he saw me and motioned me over with a wave. He was dressed in his civvies, that is, a polo shirt and khakis instead of his black shirt and collar and his dress grays. His white hair was as thick as it ever was, and he looked to be in great shape for a man in his seventies. Sparkling blue eyes looked kindly on everyone he met from behind round, tortoise-shell glasses.

"Good news," he said, smiling. "My second retirement is coming to fruition a tad early."

"Really? What's up?"

"St. Barnabas found a priest."

"That was quick. Did we use a headhunter?"

"Nope. Didn't need to."

"Well, fill me in. Who is it?"

"It's Gaylen. Gaylen Weatherall."

"She's the Bishop of Colorado," I said.

"Soon to be retired. Her father had moved out there after her mother died, but can't deal with the altitude. He's got emphysema."

"So she's coming back here? As a priest?"

"We offered her the job, and she accepted. She'll be back next month. I might add that, even though she retired from the episcopate, she's still a bishop. The Right Reverend Rector of St. Barnabas."

"That's great!" I said. "I know you're happy."

"You bet I am," said Father Tony. "I'm going to visit Wes, Carol and the kids for a few months. Did you know they moved to Florida?"

"I didn't know that, but it sounds like fun. You need to see those grandkids."

"You ain't kiddin'!"

•••

"Did you hear the news?" asked Georgia as I walked into the bookstore.

"Father Tony just told me."

"Isn't it wonderful?"

"Yeah, great. Do you have a copy of *Playback?* It's Raymond Chandler. I can't find my copy anywhere."

"No, but I can order it for you," said Georgia.

"Then do so at once, my good woman."

Georgia laughed. "It'll be here in a couple of days."

"I'll check back," I said as I turned to leave. "Thanks."

I walked out onto the sidewalk, squinted my eyes against the sun, and wondered if Meg might need a hand sorting out some rather egregious investment problem over a cup of tea.

"Chief Konig," said a voice behind me. I turned and saw Brianna Stafford standing in front of me. Her hands were clasped in front of her, resting nervously on her tennis skirt. She had a lime-green sweater draped loosely around her shoulders, and her bottle-blonde hair was tied back in a ponytail. One expensive white tennis shoe was tapping absently on the pavement.

"Brianna. How're you doing?"

103

"Okay, I guess."

"Can I help you?"

"I need to show you something. Would you come over to the house?"

"Sure. Now?"

"Uh huh. I'm just around the corner and down the street."

"Let's go, then," I said with a smile.

We walked down Main Street, away from the square, into one of the old established neighborhoods. I knew exactly where Brianna Stafford lived. Hers was one of the largest houses in the downtown area, originally built as a summer residence for an Atlanta banker. Brianna didn't say anything on our walk over. She kept her eyes facing front and her back straight, walking at a clip that I had to hustle to match.

We turned up the walk and ascended the granite steps onto the massive wrap-around porch whereupon Brianna pulled a key out of her pocket, unlocked the front door and walked into the house ahead of me. The hallway was full of boxes, sealed with packing tape and labeled with their contents.

"You're leaving?"

"I can't live here anymore. I'm moving back to Auburn. That's where my family is."

"I understand. When will you be leaving?"

"In a couple of weeks, I guess. I have some things packed up,—" she gestured toward the boxes in the hall,—"but I still have to sell the house."

"What is it you wanted to show me?"

"In here," she said.

Brianna led me into a large room off the hallway. Large shelves covered the walls, floor to ceiling, and were loaded with hundreds of books in leather bindings of various colors. I tipped one out and ran a finger over the dust on the golden page edges. *Middlemarch* by George Eliot. Unread. Probably all of them. There was a huge, overstuffed leather couch in front of a fireplace flanked by two matching arm chairs. Against one wall was an antique desk, French, by the looks of it. There were some files stacked on one end; an expensive laptop in the center; and various electronic accessories, including an iPod, a USB hub, some speakers and a large monitor that Russ could plug into if he wanted a big screen.

"This was Russ' office," she said flatly. "I was packing up his desk when I found that." She pointed to a manila envelope sitting beside the laptop. I looked at her and raised my eyebrows.

"Go ahead. Open it."

I walked over to the desk, picked up the envelope, opened it and poured five uncut diamonds onto the desk.

"Russ never told me anything about them," Brianna said. "But when I saw them I knew they were just like the ones that were in the time capsule."

"They sure look like it," I said. "There wasn't a note or anything?"

Brianna shook her head. "Do you think he stole them from St. Barnabas?" she asked in a small voice.

"No," I said. "Noylene said he was trying to buy her place. I'll bet he found them up there."

Brianna relaxed visibly. "I was so scared," she said. "I prayed they weren't from the church. We've been working with the youth group. Afterglow."

"I know. Listen, can I ask you something?"

"Okay." She was nervous again.

"There's been talk about some inappropriate behavior..."

Her face fell. "I heard some of the girls whispering about it, but when I asked, they wouldn't tell me. It wasn't Russ."

"You sure?"

She was quiet for a moment, then, "Pretty sure. We were happy. We couldn't have any kids of our own, but we were happy." She paused for a moment, then said, "You think he was killed because of those diamonds?"

"Maybe. I don't know yet." I picked up the handful of stones, uncut but hinting at brilliance that was waiting to be discovered. "What do you want to do with these?"

"Are they mine?"

"I suppose they are. We don't know where he got them for sure, so no one else has a claim to them that I can see."

"What do you think I should do?"

I shrugged. "If it were me, I suppose I'd sell them. It's a lot of money, Brianna."

She nodded sadly. "I guess I will."

Chapter 13

The two college kids looked scared. Nancy had them sitting on a couple of folding chairs with their backs to the front window. She was behind the desk typing something or other and had been letting them stew for a half-hour or so, occasionally glancing up and giving them a menacing look. I walked over and smiled at them. Bad cop, good cop.

Nancy pulled out her pad and read. "I pulled these two over just outside of town," she said. "I happened to see them loading up some stuff in the parking lot at the Baptist church. Then they failed to come to a complete stop before pulling out. James Tinsdale and John Perdue. James was driving. Truck is registered to a Charles Tinsdale. No insurance card. I didn't want to book him till you had a chat with them."

"Which one of you is John?" I asked. The tall, good-looking black kid stood up and stuck out his hand. His grip was strong, and he looked me right in the eye. Confident. The other boy stood up as well, following John's lead, but didn't offer his hand and was staring at his scuffed cowboy boots.

"I'm John Perdue."

"Chief Konig," I replied, then looked at the other kid, a scrawny fellow with long, light brown hair, wearing a faded, black Charlie Daniels Band t-shirt and almost-new jeans. "Then you must be James. Or is it Jimmy?"

He glanced up at me, then back down at the floor. "Yessir," he muttered. "Jimmy."

"C'mon in," I said. "I just have a few questions for you."

They followed me into my office and sat down in the two chairs facing my desk.

"You want a drink or something?" I asked. "We have some coffee. Or I can send Nancy to get you a Coke."

"No, thanks," said John. Jimmy shook his head.

"You heard about the murder that took place at the Bible Bazaar?"

John looked scared. "Yes, sir, we did."

"We weren't there, though," said Jimmy hurriedly, relief flooding his face.

"Hmm," I said. "I thought you were."

"You were the tax-collector, weren't you?" asked John.

"Yep. And, according to my list, you two were the Roman soldiers."

"That's right," said Jimmy, now looking at me. "But we'd already left."

I thought back. These two had been in the crowd, standing off to the side, nearest the church.

"We were there at the beginning," said John. "But we had band rehearsal at five o'clock. Miss Kendrick said we'd be finished before then, but everything was running late. It was after five when the play started."

I remembered the hostile takeover.

"We stayed as late as we could, but after it began, we snuck off," John said. "We only heard later about what happened."

Jimmy nodded, a bit too enthusiastically. "You can check with the rest of the band."

"I'll do that." I shuffled some papers on my desk for a moment. "What kind of music do y'all play?"

"We're on the praise team at church," said John. "I play keyboard and guitar and violin. Jimmy's the lead singer in our new group. We're practicing down in Boone for the 'Battle of the Country Bands.'"

"You write your own stuff?"

John gave me a big grin. "Some. I'm not as good with country songs."

I returned his grin tooth for tooth, then turned to Jimmy. "Say, you don't have any drugs in that truck, do you?"

It was a question out of left field and had the desired effect. John looked at me with a confused expression, but Jimmy went white as a ghost and dropped his gaze immediately back to his boots. His left hand started shaking, and he gripped the armrest hard, trying to stop it. I'd bet a box of donuts that there was some pot in the truck, tucked in a Baggie and stuffed down in the seat cushion or locked in the glove box.

"Here's the thing, Jimmy," I said. "You're what? Eighteen? Nineteen? You get arrested on a drug charge, you're going to be looking at time. We don't take kindly to that sort of thing here. Not only that, but John would be going to jail with you. You want that?"

It wasn't exactly true. Kids' parents had expensive lawyers, and most were quick to come to the defense of their misguided but headstrong offspring. Still, Jimmy looked like the kind of kid who might be shaken out of this kind of behavior. Besides, even if I wanted to, we couldn't search the truck without a warrant or probable cause at least, and we didn't have either.

"No, sir," muttered Jimmy, still not looking at me.

John was looking at him, incredulity written all over his face.

No more good cop. Now, I was bad cop. "Here's your one chance," I growled. "You go get your stash and you give it to Lieutenant Parsky there at the desk. You do that, and you walk out of here with a warning. That sound fair to you?"

"Yessir," said Jimmy, now visibly shaking.

"And I'll be keeping an eye out for that truck. You so much as miss a turn signal, and we'll pull you over and search that thing top to bottom. Even bring in the drug dog. And I guarantee we'll find something. Do I make myself clear?"

Jimmy shook his head in the affrmative, probably unaware that our drug-dog status was "imaginary." I glared at John who was, in turn, glaring at Jimmy, his expression having passed unbelief and quickly heading toward anger.

"Now get out of here," I said.

Jimmy left the office as quickly as he could without sprinting. Nancy hid a smile as he disappeared out the front door. He was back inside in a matter of seconds, sliding a little plastic bag across the counter toward Nancy. Then he was gone again. John, on the other hand, stood and watched him, then offered me his hand again.

"Thank you, sir," he said. "I didn't know."

"Doesn't matter whether you know or not. You watch yourself, John."

•••

"You really want a drug dog?" asked Nancy. She held up a dime bag of marijuana, twenty dollars worth on the street. "I've got one we can use."

"Yeah?"

"I've been training Sassy."

I laughed. "Sassy's a chihuahua."

"All the better. She can get into those little places that big dogs can't."

"Sassy's an *obese* chihuahua. She weighs twenty-five pounds. She can barely get into a Pizza Hut."

"Hey, let's not get into personalities."

"Okay, sure," I said. "Let's give her a try. It should give us a lot of street cred. I presume you've trained her to not eat the drugs if she finds them?"

"Of course. By the way, Jeremy and Jenny Thatcher own a little craft store in Valle Crucis." She flipped through a couple of pages in her notebook. "Crab Orchard Crafts. You want me to go talk to them?"

"Yeah. I don't think they're good for this, but run on over there and see what they have to say."

Nancy grinned. "Tomorrow morning first thing. I'll take Sassy with me. She likes to ride up front on the bike. And who knows? That craft store may be a front for a meth lab."

"By all means," I said. "But they'd have to be stuffing the drugs inside burritos for Sassy to find them."

Chapter 14

I hadn't been to Lizard Lick since the National
Convention of aught-two when I had been called in to
solve the murder of the foremost benediction composer
Hirohito Origami, who had just completed his magnum opus
--the world's first 54-fold Amen. It was an open and shut
case, and I was done and gone, my fat fee folded like a
crane and tucked in my 1662 prayerbook, before the last
"amen" bounced off the stained glass. Still, something
haunted me, haunted me like that ghost in the movie where
Patrick Swayze gets killed in a mugging, but he's still in
love with Demi Moore, and they do that thing with the wet
clay while "Unchained Melody" plays on the jukebox, but
not him--the spooky ghost in the subway. Back in aught-
two, the murmurings had already begun, murmurings of a
"Creation Museum," the kind of murmurings that linger
like the stench of a dead chipmunk in an organ pipe and
strike fear in the heart of every evolutionist with a
dinosaur bone hip replacement. The only thing slowing the
project was a lack of cash. I'd seen the plans. Building
a full-scale replica of Noah's Ark, complete with live
hippos, would take a lot of skinny.

I wasn't back in my office two minutes when there was
a knock at the door. It was Constance. Watching her walk
in was like watching two fat bulldogs that had treed a
scrawny yellow cat at the top of a flagpole that for some
reason had decided to sprout volleyballs.

"I was just down at police headquarters," she said in a
sing-songy voice that reminded me of Pat Boone's rendition
of "I Was Just Down at Police Headquarters."

"Yeah?"

"Detective Hammer said that Wiggy was poisoned."

"Poisoned?" I said.

"That's what Hammer said." She slid onto the sofa like
an extra-greasy fried egg onto a plate of hash. "Now, come
sit next to me and we'll decide what to do next."

Her bosom roiled like piglets, and as I gazed deep,
deep into the limpid brown puddles that were her eyes, I
knew she could become my soulmate if I could move beyond
one question: What was that thing on her lip?

●●●

I met Meg for lunch at The Ginger Cat. As I sipped my cup of Euthanasian Asperigo Latte or something that sounded just as ridiculous, she skimmed my latest chapter, the one I'd finished this morning after she'd left for work.

"Oh, *really!*" she huffed. "Her bosom roiled like piglets? What does that even mean?"

"A genius never elucidates his creations," I said. "Each reader will glean what truths he or she can accept. This is the way of all true artists. Did James Joyce ever have to explain his unreadable prose? Or Marcel Proust?"

"Good point," conceded Meg. "And you are the Proust of Appalachia. Okay, Monsieur Artiste, what are you having for lunch?"

"Something with mustard."

"I'm having the Pasta Puttanesca. It's today's special."

"Ah," I said. "Harlots' pasta. It sounds spicy."

"Harlots, eh? Well, if it's good enough for harlots, I guess it's good enough for me."

"Can I pull up a chair?" We both turned and saw Noylene standing a few steps from the table. Cynthia was coming up behind her, hurriedly scribbling something on her pad.

"Sure," said Meg. "Sit down. We were just about to order."

Cynthia finished writing, dropped a check down on the table next to us, and seemingly conjured a glass of water out of thin air for Noylene.

"Y'all ready to order?" she asked.

"I'll have the Harlot's special," said Meg. Cynthia looked at her blankly. "The Pasta Puttanesca." Cynthia smiled and wrote it down.

"I'll have my usual."

"Right," said Cynthia, still writing. "A mustard sandwich. You want anything else on that? Ham, maybe?"

"Yeah. Ham."

"Tomato? Lettuce? Maybe a pickle on the side?"

"Okay," I said.

"Swiss cheese? Some potato salad?"

I nodded happily.

"Rye bread okay?"

"Just right," I said.

Cynthia finished writing and turned to Noylene.

"You got any soup? I'm not feeling too perky today. Morning sickness."

"Sure, hon. We've got mushroom or enchilada."

"Better give me the mushroom," said Noylene.

"Would you like some chervil on that?"

"*What?*" said Noylene, not at all sure that she'd heard correctly. "Gerbil?"

Meg, who was unfortunately taking a sip of water, snorted some of it out her nose in a most unladylike fashion. I managed a cough.

"Yes," said Cynthia without a blink. "Gerbil. I could give it just a gentle squeeze to see if you like it or not. If you do, I'll take it back and give it a real yoink."

"Umm," said Noylene. "Okay, I guess."

"May I have a yoink of gerbil on my sandwich?" I asked.

"I don't think so," said Cynthia with a sniff. She spun on her heel, still writing, and went to turn in our order.

"So," I said to Noylene, "what's up?"

"I heard that Russ Stafford found some diamonds on my land."

"Where did you hear that?"

"Word gets around," said Noylene.

"Sorry I'm late," said Nancy, walking up and taking the empty chair. "I talked to the Thatchers. They have a cute little store over there in Valle Crucis."

"What's it called?" asked Meg.

"Crab Orchard Crafts," said Nancy.

"Oh, I've been in there," said Meg. "Mother and I stopped by a few weeks ago when we went over to the Mast General Store. It's darling."

"Did you order me anything to eat?" asked Nancy.

"Nope," I said. "I never know what to get. You might want to try the gerbil soup."

Nancy looked puzzled for a moment, then chose to ignore me and continued. "Nice couple. Two little kids. They only started going to New Fellowship Baptist a month ago. They haven't even joined the church. Jenny Thatcher says they're still 'church-shopping.' Her exact words."

"So they have no vested interest in whether New Fellowship

gets sued or not," I said. "Not really."

"Not that I can see," said Nancy. "And neither one of them seems like the murdering type."

Cynthia arrived at the table with Noylene's bowl of soup, Meg's Harlot pasta and my mustard sandwich with all the trimmings. She set them down with a waitress' practiced efficiency.

"Is that the gerbil soup?" asked Nancy. "I'll have that and a ham and Swiss on rye."

"Will do," said Cynthia. "I'll be back to refill your drinks in a sec."

"Can we get back to the diamonds?" said Noylene.

"What diamonds?" asked Nancy.

"The diamonds that Russ Stafford found on Quail Ridge."

"Oh, *those* diamonds," said Nancy.

"Well," I said, "Brianna has some raw diamonds that looked a lot like the ones that were in the time capsule. But whether Russ found them on Quail Ridge or somewhere else is anyone's guess."

Noylene gave me a smirk. "I *guess* that he found them on Quail Ridge. That's why he wanted to buy it so bad."

"You're probably right, but there's no way to prove it, Noylene. The diamonds legally belong to Brianna."

"Oh, I know. I'm just asking 'cause Wormy's been up there from morning till night for the past two weeks, looking for that cave. I'm gettin' worried about him."

"If he thinks those diamonds are up there, he may be at it for a while."

Noylene's eyes narrowed. "You don't think I killed Russ, do you? 'Cause I didn't. He may have been a snake, but I didn't kill him."

"I'll bet you thought about it, though. He was going to steal Quail Ridge from you."

"I didn't kill him."

"Relax, Noylene," I said. "I know you didn't kill him."

Meg looked over at me with a quizzical expression. Nancy hid her surprise, but waited for the explanation.

"We took that rock in for analysis the next day. There wasn't anything on it. No fingerprints, no DNA. Nothing."

"So?" said Noylene.

"That afternoon, you'd just come over from the Beautifery. You were still blowing on your nails. They weren't even dry."

Noylene smiled. "*Passionella Pink.*"

"So you couldn't have done it," said Meg happily. "There would have been nail polish on the rock."

"Some trace of it, anyway," said Nancy. She turned to Noylene. "I'm glad you're in the clear. I would have hated to find someone else to cut my hair."

"Me, too," said Noylene. "I wouldn't have had any problem killing him, though. No problem at all."

"I know," I said.

Meg and Nancy nodded their agreement.

•••

"Have you found the children a musical yet?" asked Meg, after Nancy and Noylene had finished their lunch and headed back to their respective workplaces. "You have your first rehearsal tomorrow morning. Ten o'clock, isn't it?"

"Ten o'clock to eleven thirty. And, as a matter of fact, I have. Something that will make us both happy. It's a miniature oratorio by Henry Purcell. A companion piece to *Saul and the Witch at Endor*, otherwise known as *In Guilty Night*."

"I've never heard of it."

"It's one of the compositions that Purcell enthusiasts would select as touchstones of his genius. It's really a musical dialogue in the Italian style, about twelve minutes long."

"Touchstone, eh? I love it when you start quoting from your music appreciation lectures. What's this companion piece?"

"Here's the exciting part. It's a newly discovered work. There's mention of it in the literature, of course, but no one has ever found the score."

"And?"

"And, I just got the word from Geoffrey Chester. Apparently, the score has been discovered in the library of St. Catharine's College at Cambridge among Henry Purcell's grandson's papers. They'd been left to the college when he died in 1765, but he was a minor musician at best, and no one paid them any attention."

"It seems remarkable that a composition by Henry Purcell could have been overlooked for all these years," said Meg, with more than a hint of skepticism in her voice.

"And yet," I said, "it was."

"And the name of this masterpiece?"

"*Elisha and the Two Bears,*" I said. "We'll be doing the American premiere. The world premiere will be at St. Catharine's in two weeks. We've got to hurry, though. There will be plenty of early music groups vying to be the first to perform it over here."

"How can we get the music?"

"I already have it," I said with a smile. "Geoffrey got a copy from the organist at the college and faxed it over this morning."

"I don't know the story. Are there children in it?"

"A children's chorus, a tenor, and two basses. Twelve minutes long, start to finish. A miniature opera."

"This could be just the thing to jump-start our children's choir," said Meg.

"That's what I'm thinking, too."

Chapter 15

I was usually off on Saturdays, but since I had a special children's choir rehearsal, I'd also made an appointment with Mitch St. Claire. He'd been in Winston-Salem for the last couple of days, but said he'd be happy to meet me downtown at nine o'clock. After parking my old truck in front of the police station, I had just enough time to pick up a cup of coffee and a cheese danish at the Slab. I took my breakfast into the park, found an unoccupied bench and spent a few minutes watching the Bear and Brew go up. A full crew was working, even though it was a weekend, and, at the rate they were going, the restaurant looked as though it would be back in business in a month or so. Maybe sooner.

I finished the last bit of the pastry, took a sip of coffee, and was just licking my fingers clean when I saw Mitch St. Claire and Brother Hog coming toward me across the newly mown grass.

Mitch wasn't a tall man. In fact, he was quite short, maybe five-six or seven. If he felt deficient in the height department, he certainly tried to make up for it in the gym. He had the rolling gait of a man who lifted weights incessantly and the secondary characteristics of a gym-rat who indulged in the occasional injection to improve his look and performance. I suspected he'd been in more than a few body-building competitions. He was wearing a tight, dark red t-shirt with a picture of a Herculean Jesus carrying a massive cross up a mountain. His biceps strained against the material, and I could count his abs from ten feet away. His waist was tiny and his legs stuck out of his shorts like tiny tree-trunks. He was tanned and shaved, from the top of his slick head down to his hiking boots. His right hand was in a cast, something I hadn't noticed at the Bible Bazaar, due to the beggar's cloak he'd been wearing.

"Good morning," I said.

"Morning, Chief," said Brother Hog.

I hadn't seen Rev. Hogmanay McTavish since the fire. He'd been lying low, at least as a public figure.

"Morning, Chief Konig," said Mitch, sticking out his hand. I knew what was coming, so I was proactive. Little guys with something to prove sometimes like to show off with crushing handshakes, and I wasn't a fan of having my knuckles busted. The trick is to slide your hand all the way into theirs and squeeze with equal pressure.

If they can't grind your bones for a few seconds, maybe make you wince, the showdown is over. I thought I detected a little snarl as he dropped my hand. Maybe not.

"You wanted to talk to me?"

"Just a couple of questions," I said. "I'm talking to everyone who was at the Bible Bazaar."

"You want to know if I killed Russ Stafford?"

"Well..."

"I didn't," said Mitch. "But I would have beat the hell out of him if I'd had half a chance."

"Oh?"

"You don't make a mockery out of the Word of God and walk away without consequences."

"I understand how you feel," I said. "But sometimes discretion can be the better part of valor."

"That's a load of sissy Christian crap!"

"I beg your pardon?"

"I'm the head of a mens-only Bible group called Manpower for Jesus. We don't believe in that panty-waist version of Christianity. Jesus and Paul were serious dudes. They had teeth missing. Jesus was a carpenter, and he hauled a tree up a mountain after being beaten half to death with metal whips. Paul was in prison for years. You know what prison was like in those days? These guys didn't eat tofu and bean sprouts. They didn't hang out at the country club. They were out kicking some serious heathen butt. Same thing with King David. Sure, he might have played the harp, but he made up for it by slaughtering thousands of guys. *Thousands!* In our Manpower group, we mix our Bible study with ultimate fighting."

"Is that why you got in that fight in Greenville?"

Mitch spit on the ground in disgust. "Calls himself a Man of God. Twinkie of God is more like it! He had no business leading a conference like *Jesus 2.0—Retool and Reload.* He's just some powder-puff who wears a robe and gets his nails done once a week. I told him to take his best shot or go back to playing My Little Pony with the rest of the girls."

"You told him to take his best shot?"

"Yep," said Mitch proudly. "Held out my chin and gave him a free swing."

"Did he take it?" I asked.

"Nope. That's when I hit him."

"Hard?"

"Nah. Not hard. I just wanted to wake him up to the truth."

"And your hand?"

"Well," Mitch admitted, "I broke a couple of my fingers on his face."

"A couple?"

He shrugged. "Four."

"Sounds like you hit him pretty hard."

"I pulled that punch. If I'd hit him square, he'd be dead."

I looked at Brother Hog. "It's true," he said. "I was there for the deposition."

Mitch held up his right hand and smiled at me. His four fingers were taped together and encased in plaster. "I couldn't have picked up a rock, much less beat someone to death with it."

"How about your other hand?" I asked.

Mitch held up his left hand. "I can't use three of these fingers either. Christian stick fighting league. I could have used the padded gloves—the rules allowed it— but I thought it was a spiritual compromise."

•••

I mentally checked Mitch off my list, dialed Nancy on my cell and gave her the news. We were quickly running out of suspects. I got back to my truck and heard a voice behind me.

"Chief Konig?"

I turned and saw John Perdue walking toward me.

"Hi, John," I said affably. "Can I help you with something?"

"I just wanted to let you know that Jimmy Tinsdale isn't singing with the band anymore. I won't be hanging around with him."

I nodded, but said, "Don't throw away a friend because of a mistake."

John shook his head. "He wasn't a friend, really. I don't even know how I got hooked up with him. Anyway, none of the other guys in the band liked him. He runs with a different crowd. Trouble is, he had a good voice and he was our lead singer."

"So you need a lead country singer?"

"Yeah. We really do."

"Can you use a female voice?"

John shrugged. "I guess."

"Have I got the girl for you. People have told her she sounds just like Loretta Lynn."

•••

I arrived at the church to general hubbub of the kind that always precedes a new activity. Kimberly Walnut was racing around with her clipboard, taking the names of parents, getting addresses and signing the children to what was, apparently, a long-term contract. After fifteen minutes of Kimberly's frantic activity, I took the children up to the choir room and sat them down. There were twelve of them. The members of the Gang of Five were all in attendance. In addition, Ashley's older brother Jack had come with two of his friends. Jack was twelve and a polite kid. His friends were a couple of freckled, red-headed twins named Garth and Garrett Douglas. Their father worked for the forestry service and had helped me up at the cabin several times. The other four children were third graders, a year younger than Moosey and his crew. I knew their parents, but didn't know the kids.

"Okay, everyone," I said. "Let's introduce ourselves. I'm Chief Konig."

"Can we call you Maestro?" asked Ashley, with a giggle.

"No," I said. "Chief Konig. Or Sir."

More giggles.

I pointed at them one at a time and called their names to make sure I had them right. Moosey, Bernadette, Ashley, Christopher, Dewey, Jack, Garth and Garrett. I stopped when I got to the kids I didn't know.

"Stuart," said the first boy, grinning as I pointed at him. His introduction was followed, in turn, by Mary, Jared, and Madison.

"Great," I said, playing a couple of gospel riffs that would make Bill Gaither cry. "Let's get cracking. First, we learn how to sing. Then we're going to put on an opera."

Chapter 16

"What are the chances," said Pedro, sipping his chicken liver schnapps and lighting up a stogie the size of a cucumber, "that Wiggy Newland and Constance Noring would both be registered Theological Platyputarians?"

"As slim as Oprah's size 2 Spanks," I said, lighting a stogie of my own. "Of course, the duck-billed platypus is pointed to by the creationists as the proof that evolution is a scam."

"Whether it is or whether it's not," said Pedro, "there are only three registered platyputarians in the Diocese, and they're linked together tighter than Aunt Zoomer's Ringtail Sausages."

"We've got Constance and Wiggy. Who's the third one?"

"Twelve-Fingered Teddy."

The revelation hit me like Romans 13:11. Aussi diamonds, platypuses, the Creation Museum at Lizard Lick. The answer was obvious, as obvious as Joan Rivers' last facelift.

•••

"Guess what?" exclaimed Muffy Lemieux as she adjusted the surplice over her robe. "I'm in a country band! And Varmit's gonna help out on the mixing board!"

The sopranos looked slightly startled, but smiled politely.

"That's wonderful, dear," said Georgia. "But do you think you can separate your choir singing from your solo career? I mean, won't your country stylings interfere with that certain blend we're trying to achieve?"

"Nicely put," whispered Meg.

"Oh, sure," said Muffy. "We professional singers can do different styles like crazy. Y'all can come down and hear us if all y'all want. We're gonna be at the 'Battle of the Country Bands' in a couple of weeks at the Hair o' the Dog Bar and Grill. Varmit even wrote us a new song."

"Excellent," I said. "I'm sure we'll all be happy to come out and support your efforts. But right now, let's go over the communion anthem."

"I need a summer job," said Tiff. "Any of y'all know of anything?"

Tiff was a voice major at Appalachian State and had been singing in the St. Barnabas choir for a couple of years under our "scholarship for young singers" program.

"I'm pretty sure Pete's looking for a waitress at the Slab," Meg volunteered. "Hard work, lousy hours, good tips!"

"Really?" said Tiff. "That'd be great. Can you give me a recommendation?"

"Oh, sure," said Meg. "Why don't you go on over during the sermon? You can be back by the time we have to sing the anthem."

"Hey," I said. "Hang on..."

"Here. I'll write you a quick note. Make sure you talk to Pete. He's the old hippie with the ponytail."

"Thanks!" said Tiff. "I really appreciate it."

"You be back by the gradual hymn," I growled. "And not one second later."

•••

After church, Meg and I had a leisurely picnic down by the lake. Our little mountain lake was close to town and surrounded on three sides by the Mountainview Cemetery. The cemetery didn't have an access road directly to the shore, but anyone could park on the hill overlooking the lake and walk down, and we weren't the only ones taking advantage of the warm weather. We enjoyed pork chop sandwiches, courtesy of the Slab Café, macaroni salad and the bottle of Jacob's Creek Riesling that Bud had recommended. As usual, his advice was right on the money.

"What were you watching this morning?" asked Meg. "You know, while I was getting ready. You were laughing pretty hard."

"Trinity Broadcasting Network," I said, as I unwrapped one of the sandwiches. "It was the most amazing thing. Did you know that there is biblical proof of aliens?"

"Really?"

"Well, first of all, Jesus says in the Gospel of John 'I have sheep that are not of this pen,' a clear reference to other-worldly beings. But there's other evidence as well—in the book of Jonah, specifically. It seems that Jonah wasn't swallowed by a great fish at all, but rather kept alive inside a spaceship which happened to be hiding under the water."

"Really?"

"There's corroboration directly from the scriptures."

"Okay," said Meg, taking a bite of macaroni salad. "Let's hear it."

"First of all, Jonah couldn't have stayed alive inside a fish for three days. There wasn't enough air. It's a pretty good argument, but the lack-of-air argument has been used before, and it just doesn't hold much water."

"Oh, very funny," said Meg, rolling her eyes.

"Here's the good part. Jonah says in verse 6, 'I went down to the bottoms of the mountains.' Now, how could Jonah possibly know that he was at the bottoms of the mountains if he was inside a fish? He wouldn't be able to see the bottoms of the mountains."

A quizzical look crossed Meg's face.

"Unless," I said, "and this may be the crux on which all Judeo-Christian belief hangs, *unless the fish had windows.*"

"I don't follow," said Meg. "How can a fish have windows?"

"It couldn't," I said. "You see, it wasn't a fish at all, but Jonah thought that it was since, prior to his being thrown over the side of the boat, he'd had very limited experience with alien abductions. Also, his story may have been due, in some part, to oxygen deprivation."

"When you explain it, it all seems so plausible."

"It does, doesn't it? So what Jonah thought was a giant fish was really a spaceship. With windows."

"It all makes perfect sense," said Meg.

"I'm betting it was one of those Egyptian ones that Leonard Nimoy is always jabbering on about."

"It's a good thing I only let you watch that channel on Sunday mornings," said Meg. "I wonder if I can put a parental block on it."

•••

After we finished and packed our picnic hamper back into the trunk, Meg and I drove her Lexus out to Ardine McCollough's trailer. We were greeted by the family dog, a yellow mongrel that Moosey had, for some unknown reason, named Botox. Ardine came out onto the stoop when she heard the barking, crossed her thin arms and leaned against the door jamb. We got out of the car, took turns scratching the dog's ears, and walked to the front door.

"'Afternoon, Ardine," I said.

She frowned, but didn't say anything.

"We need to talk to you and Pauli Girl," I said. "She's here, isn't she?"

"Inside," said Ardine, tossing her head in the direction of the door. "C'mon in. Bud took Moosey up to the library."

The McCollough trailer was always neat as a pin. Ardine worked hard, usually holding down a couple of jobs as well as selling her quilts at The Ginger Cat and other craft shops around the area. I had three or four of them myself. Meg and I sat down on the couch.

"Y'all want some tea?" asked Ardine. "The water's already on."

"Yes, please," answered Meg and I at the same time. Ardine took several minutes fixing our beverages and serving them to us in ancient china cups on chipped saucers.

"Thanks," I said.

"Yes. Thank you," said Meg.

Ardine sat in a rocking chair directly across from us, looked at us both for a long moment, then said calmly, "I know what yer thinkin'. I didn't do it. I'd tell you if I did."

"I expect you would," I said. "I've never known you to lie."

"Pauli Girl?" Ardine called. "Could you come on out here?"

I turned and glanced past the kitchen and down the short hallway. Pauli Girl came out of one of the bedrooms, saw us, and lost her color. Then she set her jaw, walked into the living room, and sat on the chair next to Ardine.

"You can't keep this a secret anymore," I said. "I need to know what's going on."

"We know you had a problem with someone at Afterglow," Meg said. "An adult. We can help. And we need to make sure that this doesn't happen to another girl. Maybe someone younger than you."

Pauli Girl chewed on her lip but nodded.

"Were you raped, honey?" asked Ardine. "You gotta tell us."

Pauli Girl shook her head and tears sprang to her eyes. "No."

"Did someone put his hands on you?" asked Meg.

She choked back a cry.

"Russ Stafford?" I asked.

Pauli Girl shook her head again and sobbed. After a couple of minutes, she swallowed hard, pulled her hair back from her face and looked me right in the eye, the image of her mother. "It was Mr. Flemming," she said.

•••

"That son-of-a-bitch," said Ardine, her words dripping with venom. "I'll cut him twelve ways from Sunday." We were standing back on the front porch. Pauli Girl had retreated to her room with Meg, but seemed to be better for having gotten the secret off her chest.

"You will not do anything!" I said. "I will take care of this. You understand?"

Ardine didn't answer.

"You understand?" I said again. "I'm not kidding. I'd have to lock you up, and Moosey would go into foster care. Understand?"

"Yes, I understand."

"Promise," I said.

"Fine," said Ardine, spitting out the word like it was poison. "I promise. But only if you do something about it."

"I'll take care of it this afternoon."

Meg came outside a few minutes later. "I think she'll be fine. She's a strong girl, but she was worried about the other kids finding out. I told her not to worry. That we'd deal with it."

We walked back to the car, Ardine following a couple of steps behind us.

"One other thing," I said, as I opened Meg's door for her. "What did you say to Bud during that play at the Bible Bazaar? You remember, when he walked off and left me to be baptized in his place."

Ardine shrugged. "Told him to move his truck. He was fixin' to get a ticket."

•••

I dropped Meg off at the house, called Nancy and drove my truck back into town to meet her. She was at the station when I arrived, going over a missing persons report that had just come in on the computer.

"Two hikers," she said. "They've been gone for a day and a half. They should have checked in yesterday afternoon."

"Were they hiking around here?" I asked.

Nancy looked back down at her information and shook her head. "Doesn't look like it. The forest service may want us to help look, though."

"Okay. Tell them to keep us informed. We'll be happy to help. Meanwhile, we're going to have a chat with Gerry and Wilma Flemming."

•••

Gerry and Wilma lived outside the city limits in an established subdivision of 1970s homes. They'd been members of St. Barnabas since they'd moved to town five years ago. Both Gerry and Wilma were in their early forties, part of the generation that wanted to get their careers established before having children. As a result, they had one child, a four-year-old boy named Caleb, who was enrolled in the church pre-school where Wilma worked as a volunteer three days a week. Gerry was the algebra teacher at Richard B. "Dick" Cheney High School. Their house was a split-level bungalow that had been updated and added to several times since it had been built. The lot was wooded, and an old tire swung from a large maple tree on a nylon rope.

Nancy and I went to the door and I rang the bell. Wilma answered. She had changed out of her Sunday, church-going clothes that I'd seen her in earlier, and was now wearing khakis, a white shirt, and tennis shoes.

"Hi, Wilma," I said. "Is Gerry home? We need to talk to both of you."

Wilma lost her color. "Is Caleb all right?"

"Fine, I think. Isn't he here?"

"He's at a friend's house," she said. "Come in. Gerry's in the den."

She led us to a comfortable sitting room where Gerry was reclining on an oversized sofa and watching a baseball game on an equally oversized plasma television. He smiled at us when we walked in and motioned for us to sit.

"What's up?" he said.

"Gerry," I said, "there's no easy way to say this. There's been a complaint against you."

Nancy glared at him. I looked at Wilma. She swallowed hard.

"What kind of complaint?"

"One of the girls in the Afterglow group."

"Oh, Gerry!" said Wilma in disgust. "Not again! You promised!"

"Shut up!" said Gerry, jumping to his feet. "Don't you say anything!"

"Sit down, Gerry," I said.

"Who was it this time?" said Wilma, her voice rising.

"I'm guessing that this is a pattern with you?" I said.

"I have a...a problem," said Gerry. "I've been seeing a psychologist. Wilma and I are working it out. I just like young women. There's nothing illegal about it."

"You're mistaken," Nancy said. "It *is* illegal."

"Who was it?" demanded Wilma.

"Pauli Girl McCollough," I said.

"It's her word against mine," said Gerry. "We're consenting adults."

"No, she's not," I said.

"If she says she didn't consent, she's a liar!" he said angrily.

"She's not a liar, Gerry. But it doesn't matter if she consented or not. She took an Advanced Placement class at your high school last April."

Gerry went white. "What are you talking about? She wasn't in my class."

"Doesn't matter," said Nancy. "Sure, she's seventeen. And the age of consent in North Carolina is sixteen. But there's a provision for sleazy teachers. Did you know that if a school faculty member engages in any sexual activity with *any* student that he or she can be charged with child molestation?"

"Oh, my God," said Wilma, her hand going to her mouth. She sank down next to Gerry on the sofa.

"Who else?" I said. "How many other girls in the youth group?"

Gerry shook his head. "None. I swear."

Wilma started crying, but Gerry sat still, eyes unfocused, looking straight ahead.

"Gerry," I said, getting up from my seat. "I'm going to let you turn yourself in. Present yourself at ten o'clock tomorrow morning at the Boone Police Department for booking. Needless to say, you won't be expected at St. Barnabas this evening."

•••

"Do you think he'll show up?" Nancy asked, when we'd gotten back in the truck.

"I think so," I said. "I mean, what are his choices? He doesn't seem like the type of guy to kill himself out of shame. If he runs for it, he'll have a federal warrant out on him. Whatever happens, I don't think Wilma will be sticking around too long. She might tolerate some infidelity in the guise of a psychological problem, but getting arrested for molesting a sixteen-year-old student is a whole 'nother thing."

"Yeah," said Nancy.

I started the truck and began the short trip back to the station.

"There's a downside to all this, though," I said.

"What's that?"

"We're just about out of suspects for Russ Stafford's murder."

"Well, how about Gerry? Or for that matter, Wilma?"

I raised my eyebrows.

"Maybe Russ found out about Gerry and threatened to expose him. Maybe Gerry told Wilma."

I shook my head. "Wilma didn't know about Pauli Girl. That caught her totally by surprise."

Nancy nodded. "I agree. But Gerry could have done it. And Russ certainly wasn't above blackmail."

"You're right. But how would Russ have found out about Gerry's predilection for young women? And how did he find out about Pauli Girl?"

"Would Gerry have told him? Maybe bragged about it?"

"Nope. Men don't share secrets like that."

"Would Pauli Girl have told anyone?" Nancy said.

"Nope."

"Would Wilma have told her best friend Brianna, who then told Russ?"

"She might have told Brianna about his 'problem,' but that doesn't explain how he found out about Pauli Girl."

"How about the psychologist?"

"We can look into that. They tend to be close-lipped, however."

"Hey," said Nancy, with a snap of her fingers. "What if Russ saw it happen? Maybe Gerry wasn't as discreet as he thought."

"Interesting. I need to talk to Pauli Girl again."

Chapter 17

"Good morning, Madam Mayor," I said. "Have a seat. Tell us what bodes in the world of city government."

Cynthia flopped down in a chair. She'd gotten off the early shift since Noylene and her new apprentice, Tiff, seemed to have everything well in hand. Dave and Nancy had gotten to the Slab before me and talked Pete into frying up some green tomatoes as a breakfast appetizer.

"Hi y'all," said Noylene, walking up. "This here is Tiff. I'm mentoring her."

"We've met," I said. "Morning, Tiff."

"Good morning, Chief," Tiff chirped. "What can I get y'all this morning?"

Pete came walking out of the kitchen, wiping his hands on his apron. "I suggest the Omelette Tiff. Marinated capon, asparagus and acorn cheese in an egg-white omelet."

"What on earth is acorn cheese?" asked Nancy.

"What's a capon?" asked Dave.

"And what's asparagus doing in an omelet?" I said.

"It's my idea," said Tiff. "Acorn cheese is a Welsh cheese based on an old-style Wensleydale. Firm yet crumbly. It sort of tastes like creamed caramel and crushed nuts. I had the idea yesterday afternoon when I was mopping the floor." She wrinkled up her nose and shrugged apologetically. "My mom owns the cheese store in Little Switzerland. I ran down there this morning before work. She had some marinated capon left over from a wedding reception she catered so I went ahead and brought it with me."

"I see a bright future for this young lady," said Pete, proudly. "We're going to be the talk of the town. The Ginger Cat ain't gonna have nothing on us." He sat down and popped a fried tomato into his mouth.

"That omelet sounds good to me," I said. Everyone else at the table agreed.

"I'll get y'all some coffee right away," said Tiff, bouncing away.

"Capon?" said Dave.

"Castrated rooster," said Pete. "Very tender."

"She's my protegé," Noylene whispered. "The mentor-protegé relationship is a sacred bond." She followed Tiff into the kitchen.

"On a totally different subject," said Cynthia, "the City Council is made up of idiots!"

"Well, that much is a given," I said. "Only an idiot would want the job, much less spend money to be elected."

"One of them found out about the moratorium on parking tickets, and they want me to make you start giving them out again. I think it's just because out-of-towners have been parking in George Romanski's parking space."

"Okay," I said. "Tell them we will."

"Really?" said Cynthia in surprise. "I thought you would have put up more of a fight than that."

"Nah," I said. "Happens every year. Don't give it another thought."

Cynthia looked at me, then smirked. "You're not going to give out parking tickets, are you?"

"If we find a car illegally parked," said Nancy, "we'll give 'em a ticket."

"Right," said Dave. "But they're sneaky. Sometimes they'll park for a few hours, then drive around the block, and park right in the same place. It's almost impossible to catch them."

Cynthia laughed. "Okay, I'll tell the City Council you will be doing everything in your power to catch and punish these miscreants."

"That's the ticket!" I said.

"Very funny," said Cynthia.

•••

Our asparagus and acorn cheese omelets were fantastic and much better fare than we were used to at the Slab Café.

"What do we do now?" said Dave, as he finished the last bite of his breakfast. "I feel like we should applaud or something."

"Maybe we should leave Tiff a big tip?" suggested Nancy. "That was really good!"

"I think you should," said Cynthia. "Waitresses live on tips." She turned to me. "By the way, how's the murder investigation going?"

"Just great," I grumbled.

"We should have it solved by lunch," said Nancy.

"Excellent! Well, I've got to go," said Cynthia, standing up and giving Pete a kiss on the cheek. "See you tonight." Pete nodded.

"How's it really going?" asked Pete.

"Terrible," I said. "There's something we're missing."

"You went back and talked with Pauli Girl?" asked Nancy.

"Yeah, I did."

"What did she say?" asked Dave.

"She said Gerry Flemming attacked her in his car. He was giving some of the kids a ride home, and Pauli Girl was the last to be let off. He pulled off the road just before he got to her trailer. No way Russ could have seen that."

"So," said Pete. "Run it down for me. Maybe it'll help to talk it out."

"This is official police business, Pete. Confidential. You're not the mayor anymore."

"Yeah, yeah. Whatever. So run it down."

I shrugged, reached into my shirt pocket and pulled out the pad I'd taken to carrying, chiefly to keep track of all the suspects. "Here's what we've got," I said. "Russ Stafford was killed on Wednesday afternoon at about 5:10. He was playing the lead role in Kimberly Walnut's play entitled *The Stoning of Stephen,* the culmination of the action being an actual stoning by the children and adults present, using special styrofoam rocks. Unfortunately for Russ, he had an enemy somewhere in the crowd, and that person took the opportunity to drop a real rock on Russ' head while he was pretending to be dead. He wasn't pretending very long."

"Time of death, 5:15 p.m.," said Nancy.

"Gerry Flemming was the one who came and got us. We'd all gone into the temple tent for the final ceremony."

"So, who are the suspects?" Pete asked.

"Russ was not well-liked," I said.

Pete laughed. "That's the understatement of the year!"

"He was suing New Fellowship Baptist Church for burning down the Bear and Brew. Their only defense would have been that 'No, God doesn't answer specific prayer requests.' I'm not sure they would have wanted to do that. They might have settled the lawsuit quietly, but knowing Russ, he would have dragged them through a very public briar patch. Brother Hog had motive, but he wasn't there. The other Baptists who were at the Bible Bazaar were two college kids who left for band practice as soon as the skit started, a militant Testostero-Christian named Mitch St. Claire, Diana Terry..."

"The nun?" asked Pete.

"The very one," I said. "Jeremy and Jenny Thatcher and Vera Kendrick, the children's minister. The only one we haven't excluded is Vera."

"She couldn't have done it," said Dave. "She was my Sunday School teacher in sixth grade. She cried when the goldfish died."

"I don't think she did it, either," I said. "She's still on the list, though."

"So it wasn't one of the Baptists," said Pete. "Cross off 'Holy Indignation' as a motive."

"Other people that might have had a motive, but that we've eliminated, include Noylene, Brianna Stafford and Ardine or Pauli Girl McCollough."

"Who's left?" asked Pete.

"Gerry Flemming," I said. "But it's a stretch. He might have done it, but the only motive might be if Russ were blackmailing him, and there's no evidence of that."

"How about Wilma?" asked Dave.

"Don't think so," I said, and Nancy nodded in agreement. "She didn't know anything about Gerry and Pauli Girl."

"Can we look at his bank records?" asked Nancy. "Do we have enough probable cause for a warrant?"

"Indeed we do," I said. "Call Judge Adams."

Chapter 18

Gerry had presented himself at the Boone P.D. promptly at ten o'clock to be arrested. Nancy had gone down to fill out the paperwork. Wilma was not in attendance. He was arraigned and released later that evening on a seventy-five thousand dollar cash bond. He wrote a check for the full amount.

The Flemmings' bank account proved more interesting than we'd thought, but included no large withdrawals in the past month, save for Gerry's bail. Certainly nothing that indicated any blackmail payments. The case was set to be heard in July, and the word around the pre-school was that Wilma was packing up the house.

Nancy gave a $1000 parking ticket to an obnoxious couple from New Jersey who asked if they could speak to a *real* officer when she told them to move their Winnebago out of Sterling Park. The City Council was thrilled.

Other than that, the week was slow.

•••

"You better get down here," said Detective Jack Hammer when I picked up the blower that was doing its best to jangle itself off the desk. "We've got another stiff. A friend of yours."

"Yeah? Who?"

"Guy named Teddy. Teddy Rupskin."

"He have twelve fingers?"

"Hang on a sec. I'll count 'em."

I waited for a few moments, letting my thoughts drift to Constance. I liked my Australian women the way I liked my kiwi fruit, sweet yet tart, firm of flesh, yet yielding to the touch, and covered with short brown fuzzy hair. Constance Noring was perfect in so many ways and yet...

"Yeah, twelve," said a voice filled with sufficient gravel to cover all the dirt roads in Watauga County with enough left over to re-pave Bea Arthur's vocal chords. "He crashed his Vespa into the front of Buxtehooters. But my guess is, he was dead before the scooter hit the building."

"I'll be there soon as I can," I said. "Be careful when you frisk him. Chances are, he's got a platypus in his pants."

•••

"I just read that Elisha story!" said Meg, in her horrified voice. "You are *not* doing that with our children's choir."

"It's too late, my pet," I said. "The children already know it and love it. Moosey has his solo memorized, the soloists have been hired, I've ordered the bear costumes, and the publicity machine is running rampant across the tar heel state."

"But the bears eat the children!"

"Yes, but with good reason."

"Good reason? They called Elisha 'baldhead.' That's hardly justification for Elisha to have his bears kill all the children."

"They were youths," I said. "Not children. *Youths*. It was a youth group."

"Oh," said Meg. "Well...a youth group. That explains it."

•••

"Very good," I said. "One more time through, and I think you'll have it."

The children's choir was doing very well, and I was enjoying it more than I thought I would. *Elisha and the Two Bears*, the newly-discovered Henry Purcell masterpiece, had two choruses for the children as well as a lovely solo aria to be sung by Moosey. The other roles were for a tenor, portraying the prophet Elisha, and two basses—the bears. I'd had auditions for the solo, but it was no contest. Moosey had been listening to my snooty English choirboy CDs for years and was an excellent mimic.

"When do we get to hear the bears?" asked Dewey.

"Next week. We're going to need a couple of extra rehearsals, but I think we'll be ready to perform this a week from tomorrow."

"Are we going to sing this during church?" asked Bernadette.

"Yes," I said. "In place of the sermon. I've already cleared it with Father Tony."

"Are we selling tickets?" asked Garth. "Mom said she'd take six."

"No tickets," I said. "Everyone's invited."

"Can we sing that part about 'broken limbs and faces faire' again?" asked Madison. "That's my favorite song."

"Mine, too!" said Stuart. "That's the part where we all get chewed up by the bears!"

With broken limbs and faces faire,
Now supper for the ancient bear,
We moan the curse that sealed our fate,
The mocking of his balding pate.

Chapter 19

"Choir practice is our social activity for the week," said Meg. "You can't expect us to shut up and sing."

"Anyway, we're off this Sunday," said Marjorie. "The kids are doing their musical."

"Yeah," said Marty, "so stop bothering us."

"Do you think we might rehearse just a bit?" I asked. "I'll let you sing something sweet. Maybe something by John Rutter."

"Which one?" asked Georgia, suddenly interested. "Not one of those Renaissance re-mixes!"

"How about *A Gaelic Blessing*?" I offered.

"Nah," said Bev. "What about *For the Beauty of the Earth*?"

"Too many notes," I said.

"I like that one about sweet, sweet music," said Marjorie.

"That's a Christmas anthem," said Meg.

"*A Clare Benediction? God Be In My Head? The Lord is My Shepherd?*"

"That last one," said Fred, perking up. "It's the one with the oboe, right?"

"Yeah," I said. "I just happen to have the copies right here."

You fools, I thought, laughing to myself in my Vincent Price voice. *You've played right into my hands.* I knew they'd go for the 23rd Psalm. Now I had them right where I wanted them.

"Tell us about this musical," said Bob Solomon. "I hear that it's an American premiere."

"Absolutely right," I said. "Although Henry Purcell is an English composer."

"Old-timey?" asked Marjorie.

"Born in 1659," I said, "and died at age thirty-five. The manuscript was found at Cambridge earlier this year."

"What's it called?" asked Randy. "You've been rehearsing those kids like crazy!"

"*Elisha and the Two Bears.*"

"Is that a Bible story?" said Tiff.

"Elisha is a fine character in the Old Testament, but he didn't make it onto many Sunday School flannel-boards. His stories are sort of..."

"Gruesome?" offered Meg.

"Horrific?" said Bev.

"Grisly?" added Elaine.

"Bloodthirsty?" chimed in Rebecca.

"No," I said. "I was going to say *harsh, but fair*. This is a story to warm the hearts of follically-challenged men everywhere."

"Let's hear it," said Sheila.

"Elisha, God's prophet, just cleaned up Jericho's water supply and was on his way up to Mt. Carmel when some youths came out and made fun of him saying, 'Go on up, baldy!'"

"Nice kids," snorted Steve DeMoss. "Sounds like those hooligans over in Sterling Park."

"Those were *not* hooligans," said Sheila. "Those were eight-year-olds playing kick-the-can, and you were in their way."

"Still..." grumbled Steve, smoothing his two hairs back into place.

"Anyway, Elisha was not amused," I continued. "He called down a curse, and two bears came out of the woods and ate forty-two of them."

"What?" said Marjorie. "Ate them?"

"Amen," said Mark. "Harsh, but fair."

"That's in the Bible?" asked Tiff.

"Oh, Elisha's in some good stories," I said. "Like the one where there's a famine so bad that a quarter piece of dove dung was selling for five pieces of silver, and a donkey head was going for the equivalent of a three bedroom house."

"And?" said Rebecca.

"And this woman made a pact with her best friend that they should eat their kids. But after they ate the first one, the second woman backed out on the deal."

"Well," said Mark with a shrug. "Presumably, she was full."

"Then the king blamed Elisha for the famine and was going to cut off his head, so Elisha called the whole famine thing off."

"How come we never heard of these stories?" asked Muffy.

"Then there's the one where the woman drives a tent-peg through her husband's best friend's ear."

"Do you have a musical for that, too?" asked Meg.

"I could write one," I offered. "The grand finale would be *The Whacking Chorus*."

"Whack, whack, whack," chanted the men.

"Oh, just stop it," said Meg. "Shouldn't we be rehearsing?"

•••

Muffy Lemieux stood up to make an announcement. "I hope all y'all are going to come up to hear us at the Hair o' the Dog Bar and Grill in Boone. We'll be performin' Varmit's new song at the 'Battle of the Country Bands' on Saturday night."

"Why don't we make it a road trip?" Phil said. "We could meet here, and some of us could drive over."

This met with general agreement and enthusiasm.

"The show starts at eight," said Muffy. "Don't y'all be late. And don't get drunk before y'all vote. We're the third band to play."

•••

"Any breaking news on our murderer?" Dave asked, as he decided which donut would be voted most likely to quell his mid-morning munchies.

"Not unless someone came in and confessed while I was writing parking tickets," I said.

"Are you writing parking tickets?" asked Nancy.

"Nah," I said. "Did anyone come in and confess?"

"Nah," said Nancy.

"I still think that I'm missing something. Something important. It's right in front of us."

"We still think that Gerry did it?" asked Dave.

"Well," I said, "we can't prove it, that's for sure. And frankly, no. No, I don't think he did."

"That doesn't leave us with a lot of suspects," said Nancy. "We've looked at almost everyone that was at the Bible Bazaar. You don't think one of the kids killed him, do you?"

"Holy smokes!" said Dave. "I hope not."

"No prints on the rock," I said. "No DNA either." I shook my head. "I don't think it was a kid."

•••

I had a friend named Bucky James who was the head of the tourism council in Gatlinburg, Tennessee. Bucky and I went to high school together, and we'd managed to keep in touch over the years. In fact, I'd played the organ at his first and third weddings. I called Bucky because the Gatlinburg Tourism Council had spared no expense in creating the best bear costumes money could buy. These costumes weren't for rent, and no one was allowed to borrow them, but Bucky had found himself at a cock fight in Watauga County late one night, with no friends and the feds banging on the door. He'd needed a favor then, and I didn't mind calling one in now.

"When can you pick them up?" asked Bucky.

"Is Friday okay?" I said.

"That should be fine," said Bucky. "I need them back on Monday. Queen Margrethe II of Denmark is coming over to Dollywood, and the mayor wants to have the bears walking around all day in case she heads over this way for some miniature golf or something."

"I'll get them back to you Sunday night."

I borrowed a harpsichord from Ian Burch and moved the altar toward the front wall to give ourselves a bit more playing area. Meg and Cynthia finished the costumes, and our last dress rehearsal was scheduled for Saturday morning.

Chapter 20

Pedro met me at the Noring mansion just a little before two.

"I talked to Hammer," he said. "Twelve-Fingered Teddy had a platypus, sure enough. How did you know?"

"I figured it out. Let's get Constance and get out of here before it all shakes loose. I'll fill you in later."

The door was open and we walked into the hallway. I called her name. No answer. It was as though she'd gone on a European vacation—without taking any luggage, leaving the front door open, forgetting to notify the mailman, and not canceling her newspaper—so not really.

We found her in the library, reclining on the davenport and draped in diamonds: a diamond tiara on her head, a diamond choker around her goose-like neck, diamond bracelets on both wrists and six diamond rings the size of golf-balls. She was cold, cold as the ice she was wearing.

"Poison," I said, pointing to the wriggling mass beneath her frock. I reached under the clothes, pulled out a platypus by its tail, and held it up for inspection.

"Nature's anomaly," I said. "The Creator's little joke. Webbed feet, fur, a beaver tail, a duck-bill, a pouch, and, to add to the fun, these little rascals lay eggs."

"So how was she poisoned?" asked Pedro, glaring at the squirming creature the way a librarian looks at that guy who just comes in to read the newspapers.

"Did I forget to mention? These guys also have poison spikes," I said, pointing to the rear feet of the squirming varmint. "They're so darn cute, I guess she forgot about the poison spikes. Rookie mistake. I've seen it happen a hundred times."

"So, she and Wiggy..."

"Yep," I said. "Twelve-Fingered Teddy was in on it, too."

I reached into the pouch of the little duck-mole and pulled out a handful of diamonds and a thumb-drive. "They were smuggling the diamonds in the pouches of the platypodes. Aussi diamonds, to pay for the construction of the Creation Museum. Then they were giving these snappers away as pets to upscale Episcopalian dayschools to teach them the folly of Darwinian evolution."

"Ingenious," said Pedro. "And the thumb-drive?"

"Wiggy's files. I'll make a copy just in case, then turn it over to the Bishop and collect our fee."

"But who killed them?"

"Accidents," I shrugged. "You can't keep a platypus in your pants without consequences. Just ask Bill Clinton."

•••

The bear costumes were superb. Teeth and claws, realistic enough to make Queen Margrethe II reach for her scatter-gun. The face of the person inside was right at the base of the bear's neck, hiding behind a piece of black netting that would conceal his features, while the neck and head of the fierce beast soared upward to reach seven and a half feet in height. The fur was black and thick and actually smelled as if it came off a bear. I suspected that these costumes hadn't been cleaned for a while.

I had hired two basses for the roles of the bears. One was a voice teacher at Appalachian State by the name of Zeb Martin. He had a huge, dark voice and had sung opera in Germany for a number of years before coming back to the States to teach. The other was a Presbyterian church choir director from Greenville. Darius Reeves had a fine voice as well and had welcomed the opportunity to skip out during his church's Youth Mission Sunday. I'd heard both of them at a performance of Handel's *Israel in Egypt* in the fall where the only singing for the bass soloists is a duet that brings down the house. Almost literally. No delicate singing here. It's a contest to see which bass will remain standing at the end. By the time *The Lord Is A Man of War* has finished, if there isn't plaster loose on the ceiling, someone hasn't been doing his job. I expected no less from my bears.

The tenor was Dr. Cleamon "Codfish" Downs, a retired voice teacher who, in his 60s, still had a pretty good high 'G.' Codfish supplemented his retirement income by selling fish, stolen from a local fish farm, out of his trunk. It wasn't uncommon to hear *Nessun dorma* while buying a brace of purloined rainbow trout. I'd cornered him on Old Chambers, bought some freshwater shrimp, and talked him into playing the part of Elisha.

The kids were dressed in their Bible Bazaar 31 A.D. tunics, although gussied up just a mite with leather lacings and actual sandals in place of flip-flops. There were props as well—a few of Kimberly Walnut's styrofoam rocks for tossing, plenty of red ribbon to represent blood, and some goatskin flasks that the boys simply could not do without.

I'd tuned the harpsichord, Cynthia was on hand to supervise her choreography for the *Munching Dance*, Meg was standing by in case of a costume emergency, and we were good to go.

•••

"It's not that difficult to sing in this bear suit," said Zeb. "But I can't really hear anything. There's fur in my ears."

"It's going to be a problem," agreed Darius.

"Yeah," I said. "I didn't think of that."

"Hey," said Dave, who had wandered into St. Barnabas to watch. "I can fit you both with a Bluetooth, sync them to my Blackberry and set it on the harpsichord. You'll be able to hear the accompaniment as well as the other voices."

"Will that work?" I asked.

"Sure," said Dave with a shrug. "Why not? I'm going to run down to the Radio Shack. I'll be back in thirty minutes."

"There's a phone call for you," called Meg from the back. "On the church phone."

"I'll be right back," I said. "You kids go over your dance."

•••

"Mr. Konig?" said the voice. "My name is Dr. Hiram Milligan. I'm the president of the North American Purcell Society."

"Ah, yes. Dr. Milligan."

"Call me Hiram."

"Certainly, Hiram."

"I read in the *Boston Globe* that your early music ensemble was performing a newly discovered work."

"The *Boston Globe*?"

I heard the rustling of a newspaper. "Well, it's an AP article. St. Germaine, North Carolina. Is that correct?"

"Well, yes," I said.

"A Ms. Kimberly Walnut is quoted as saying that this newly-discovered work is the find of the century."

I gritted my teeth as I remembered saying those exact words to Kimberly Walnut not three weeks ago.

"Could you tell me something more about it? The story is from Second Kings? It says here that it may be a companion piece to *Saul and the Witch at Endor*."

"Well, possibly," I said. "It's about the same length, although there's a children's chorus in addition to the three principal voices. It was discovered at Cambridge."

"Yes, it says that here as well. At St. Catharine's College, among Henry Purcell's grandson's papers. I'm amazed that no one ever thought to look there. Well, we're all very excited here at the Purcell Society. And we can't wait to hear it."

"Hear it?" I said.

"Oh, yes! We're flying in to Greensboro tonight. Then driving up for the performance tomorrow morning. It's not every day we get to hear an unknown Purcell masterpiece."

•••

"That was the Purcell Society," I whispered to Meg. "They're coming from Boston to hear the performance tomorrow."

Meg smiled. "Well, I guess that puts you in a bit of a pickle, doesn't it?"

"What do you mean?" I asked innocently.

"Well, how are you going to explain away the fact that *you're* the one who wrote it?"

"Huh?"

Meg laughed. "It just serves you right. *Elisha and the Two Bears,* indeed!"

"You mean, you knew?"

"The *Munching Dance?*" She laughed again. "With broken limbs and faces faire? It has Hayden Konig stamped all over it."

"Well, in my defense, I didn't write all of it. Most of the music was by Geoffrey."

"Well, *that* should go over well with the Purcell Society."

•••

Meg and I rendezvoused with our group at the Hair o' the Dog Bar and Grill just before eight o'clock. Nancy had shown up, having received a personal invitation from Varmit. She'd brought Dave along as her designated driver. Many of the choir had shown up in support of Muffy and her vocal stylings. Marjorie had arrived early, sequestered a couple of tables in the back, and was sipping a chocolate martini. We paid our cover charge, found our seats and ordered the Hair o' the Dog appetizer—baked potato skins with a sour cream and some kind of salsa—and drinks. I decided to try the Rogue Shakespeare Stout. Meg ordered a glass of white wine.

"The Battle of the Country Bands" was a nice way of saying "Welcome to our talent show." The first group up was introduced as "The Kidney Stones." They weren't country in the way that Johnny Cash was country, but more of a rockabilly band. The first song, titled *Heaven's Just a Sin Away,* brought the crowd to its feet. Most of it anyway. I suspected that The Kidney Stones had quite a claque in place. Their second number was a more raucous selection—*I Wanna Whip Your Cow.* Again, the crowd showed its appreciation.

The second band on the schedule was billed as "The Bluegrass Tommys." It was a swell hook—a few guys, all named Tommy, playing bluegrass. If they were any good at all, they couldn't miss. Unfortunately, The Bluegrass Tommys didn't show up. So much for the hook.

It took a couple of minutes for Muffy and the Goat Wranglers to get their equipment set up. John Perdue was playing fiddle and guitar. The rest were college-aged guys on electric bass, drums, the pedal steel, and piano. Five of them in all, plus Muffy. The pedal steel guy also had a guitar. He and John would be switching off. Varmit was running the sound.

Muffy was wearing her signature light-green angora sweater and white capri pants. The rest of the band were in beat-up cowboy hats; embroidered western shirts, worn untucked for casual effect; and faded jeans. Their first song was *I'm the Only Hell My Mama Ever Raised,* and it was a good one. There was a fiddle break in the middle that John positively tore into. He and the bass player were also singers and good ones. Meg looked over at me in surprise.

"They're excellent!" she said.

"When you're right, you're right," I agreed.

"C'mon," said Nancy, grabbing Dave by the hand. "Let's dance."

By the time the song was over, half the crowd was on the dance floor. John finished the song with a virtuosic rip, and the crowd cheered and stomped their feet in appreciation.

"Thank you," said Muffy, into the microphone. "This next song was written by my man. He's sittin' there in the back. Say 'hello,' Varmit!" She pointed back to the soundboard and Varmit raised an embarrassed hand.

"It's called *My Skin Always Crawls Back To You,* and it goes something like this..."

The band began the intro—a slow, rolling, bluesy tune.

In south Louisiana, in the swamp, down by a stream,
I met you in the mornin', you were looking like a dream.
Then an armadillo bit you, now you're feelin' pretty mean;
But I'll never, never leave you, even if you are unclean.

The drummer counted off the beat, the tempo kicked up, and the band was rocking.

Now you've got a slight condition,
you're not feeling in the pink.
It takes some getting used to, but I can't believe you think
A little case of leprosy would cause our love to shrink;
And my skin always crawls back to you.

You're always mighty frisky
when I come on through that door,
But I never know what body parts are layin' on the floor.
My friends, they tell me not to hang around you anymore,
But my skin always crawls back to you.

Back to you, back to you, It's all that I can do,
Cause my skin always crawls back to you.

I kiss you in the morning, but I have to do it quick,
I kiss you in the evening, when we're dancing back to hip,
but how can I get all your love with half a lower lip?
And my skin always crawls back to you.

The dance floor was full again, most of the people doing a two-step, but a good number of them having already invented the "Leprosy Line Dance." I suspected that it just was a minor variation of one of the hundreds of line dances that were popular in country and western bars all over the south, but it was impressive, nevertheless.

I come home to a welcome, and I smell your after-shave;
I have to do the smelling, cause your nose they couldn't save.
You pour a couple fingers and a glass of whiskey, too.
And my skin always crawls back to you.

The chorus was coming around again, and now there were even more people on the dance floor, including most of our group. In fact, only Meg, Marjorie, and I were still sitting.

"You want to dance?" asked Meg.

"I'll give it a try," I said. "But not in that line thingy. I can just about manage a two-step."

"How about you, Marjorie?" asked Meg as we got up. "You want to join us?"

"Nope," said Marjorie. "You kids go ahead."

I kiss you in the morning, but I have to do it quick,
I kiss you in the evening, when we're dancing back to hip,
but how can I get all your love with half a lower lip?
And my skin always crawls back to you.

The last verse came around and the whole bar was jumping. I could see how this could be very intoxicating to someone who wanted to make a living on the stage. Muffy was in her element, and the rest of the band was grinning like a bunch of Cheshire cats.

I find you fascinating though I think you will agree,
That now you're only half the man that you used to be.
A leper cannot change his spots,
I've caught them, don't you see?
Now your skin always crawls back to me.

By the time the last chorus finished, there wasn't any doubt who was going to win the two hundred dollar prize. I just felt sorry for the next band up. The Ambersons were a family band from Banner Elk, consisting of the father playing a guitar, the mother on autoharp, and two sisters singing harmony and playing the spoons. They specialized in mountain gospel.

"I didn't know you danced," said Nancy, falling into her chair and downing her beer in two gulps.

"I don't," I said.

"He just did it for me," said Meg. "That's true love."

"Great song!" Dave said to Muffy as she walked up to the table.

"It was Varmit's idea," she said, still glowing from her experience. "He read this article about armadillos in Louisiana. Did you know they can carry leprosy? They're the only animal that can, except for humans. Not only that, but there's still a leper colony down there somewhere."

"I *did* know that," Dave said. "Read it in a *National Geographic.*"

"Well, it was fabulous," said Meg. "I think you guys should play in Sterling Park sometime. People would love it. What do you think, Hayden?"

I blinked. Then blinked again.

"Hayden?" Meg said. "Are you okay?"

"Son of a gun," I said. "Of course. Leprosy! I know who did it. I know who murdered Russ Stafford."

Nancy looked at me. "Dadgummit! I thought I was going to get to solve this one."

Chapter 21

"Here's what I need you to do," I said to Nancy, on what promised to be a beautiful Sunday morning. "You've got to go and make an arrest."

"Be happy to," said Nancy. I'd given her a call just before we left the house and asked if she could meet me in the parish hall. "Russ Stafford was a weasel, sure enough, but we can't have our citizens being pummeled to death with rocks during Bible School."

"No, you don't understand," I said. "I need you to set up outside of town and detain the Purcell Society before they make it in to church."

"Huh?"

"It's a long story. But they'll be coming in on Highway 68 from Greensboro."

"You want me to arrest the whole Society?"

"Well, there's probably only going to be three or four of them. Don't really arrest them. Just make sure they're occupied for a few hours. They'll be in a rental car."

"What are you two talking about?" asked Meg, as she walked up. She handed me a cup of coffee.

"Hayden wants me to arrest the Purcell Society."

"Oh, no you don't!" said Meg.

"It's for the good of the town, Meg," I argued.

"I won't hear another word! Now you get in there and tune the harpsichord. It sounds as though Lurch has been banging on it."

•••

Zeb and Darius, the two bears, had shown up early like the professionals they were. By the time all the kids had arrived and donned their Hebrew garb, the two basses had warmed up, gotten into their costumes and gone through their duet with Zeb's wife, Clarice, accompanying them on the piano. Codfish was in his costume as well, but after running through his aria, he disappeared into the parking lot to give Stuart's grandfather a great deal on some farm-raised perch.

"Moosey brought his frog with him!" said Mary. "Eeew!"

"Don't be such a tattletale," said Moosey. "That's just Ribbet.

He's in my pocket. I couldn't leave him at home. Pauli Girl's cleaning the house."

"Okay," I said. "Line up on the steps. Let's do our warm-ups. We'll only have time to go through this once before the service."

"This Bluetooth works great," said Zeb, fiddling with the Borg-like object protruding from his ear. "I'm going to remember this when we do *Love for Three Oranges* next year."

"Do we have time to rehearse the dance?" asked Cynthia. "It would be good to go through it once more."

Moosey's frog let loose a tremendous "Braaaaap!"

"Eeew!" squealed Mary, as the boys rolled on the floor, laughing.

"Moosey!" I said. "Give Meg the frog."

"I don't want the frog," said Meg.

"Well..." I looked around. "Put him in the piano bench. He'll be fine."

"Ye dreadful bears to me draw nigh and hear a Prophet's awful cry!" sang Codfish from the back of the church.

This brought more giggles from the chorus and smiles from everyone else.

"Let's warm up," I said. "Then do our run-through."

•••

"Hayden! Great to see you again!"

"Well, I do declare," I said. "Gaylen Weatherall!"

"Congratulations! I heard you'd gotten married."

"I did, indeed. What are you doing here? I didn't think you'd be arriving till sometime next month."

"I brought Dad back early. He's going into an assisted living facility in Boone, so there wasn't any sense in his staying out in Colorado and being miserable." She tapped on her chest. "Emphysema," she said.

"Sorry to hear it."

"He smoked for forty years, then finally quit, but it was too late, I guess."

"I know you'd have liked to stay out there for a while."

"Yes, I would have, but these things happen. I'm still a bishop."

"So I gathered. I guess we'll be the only parish in the country with a bishop as our rector."

"I'll have to check on that, but you may be right. Is Meg here?"

I pointed to the choir loft. "Up there, I think. We're doing a special musical presentation this morning."

"I heard. I can't wait to see it."

•••

For a Sunday in late June, the crowd for the service was pretty good. Attendance at St. Barnabas tended to go down in the summer months and back up in the winter when people were more likely to contemplate their own mortality. Nothing like a minus-ten degree windchill to freeze the immortal soul. When it was seventy-five degrees and beautiful out, it was easy to believe that God could be found anywhere, and that you'd just as likely encounter him on one of Watauga County's fine golf courses as you would sitting in a stuffy old church.

The opening hymn was *Be Thou My Vision,* and the adult choir processed up to the front, back down the side aisle and up into the choir loft. I had to play the *Gloria,* then make my way down to the front for the performance. Before the kids made their entrance, we'd hear the Old Testament lesson and the Gospel reading. The first lesson is the story of Elisha, of course, but read from the beginning of the chapter. The lectionary readings all end just before the bears show up. Odd, that. The rest of the Old Testament lesson was the reading for Transfiguration Sunday. Elijah is whisked away in a fiery chariot and Elisha, his disciple, remains with a "double-portion" of God's grace. Then, a couple of verses later, he cleans up the water supply and wreaks havoc on the Bethel youth group.

The readings were duly proclaimed and it was time for the kids to come down the aisle to the sombre tones of the overture. I looked around the church, searching for members of the Purcell Society, and spotted four faces in the back that I hadn't seen before. Bingo! Three men dressed in rumpled suits and a middle-aged woman wearing a hat. I gave them a nod.

The only instrumentation for the piece was the harpsichord. The instrument was a nice one, handmade by Ian Burch, with a big, ringing sound. There would be no problem hearing it. At least, I thought, as long as the bears' Bluetooths were working.

As the children reached the front steps, Codfish Downs, Zeb Martin and Darius Reeves, all standing in the back, sang the first trio.

Elisha, prophet, man of God,
The Fertile Hills of Judah trod.
God's judgement to these Hills did tell,
Until vile youths upon him fell.

I glanced back over my shoulder and saw Codfish coming up the aisle. With his grizzled beard and lack of hair, he looked every bit the crazed prophet, due for a taunting.

The kids sang:

Go up, thou Baldhead, yea go up.
Take thy mantle, take thy cup,
And to the birds now prophesy.
We find your preaching very dry.

Go up, thou Baldhead, grant us ease.
O prating prophet, take thy leave.
These stones we throw to fire thy shame,
And send thee back to whence thou came!

"Braaaaap," went the frog. I looked over at the piano. The lid to the bench was up just about an inch and the frog was struggling out, its amphibious body squashed almost flat as it pulled itself through the opening with webbed fingers and elbows. Its head, not able to fit easily through the crack, was twisted in a grotesque fashion, and its mouth was hanging open, revealing a blackish tongue that dangled lewdly, as it wriggled to free itself.

Thou wretched youths, sang Elisha. *I shall now hie,*
To yonder cave, where Ursine Brethren lie.

The frog popped free and landed on the slate floor with a plop like the sound of a three-pound, uncooked meatloaf being dropped on the kitchen floor. The kids all looked over at the noise. Mary grabbed Ashley's hand and made a horrible face.

Elisha continued:

Awake, awake shake off dull sleep,
awake from slumber, dark and deep.

Ye dreadful bears to me draw nigh
And hear a Prophet's awful cry.
These viperous youths, their mocking scorn,
Shall come to naught this cursed morn.

Billy Hixon, the head usher, had been sitting in the front pew, due to the fact that he was mostly deaf and also liked a good show. He heard the frog splat when it hit the slate—a testament to the sheer volume of it—and hadn't quite decided if, being head usher, he was required to corral the frog and banish it from the proceedings. He was pretty sure it wasn't part of the show, but he thought he remembered frogs in the Bible somewhere. While he was pondering this, the bears entered.

Awake, awake! Make ready then your bitter tomb,
The prophet now has sealed your doom!

The effect was startling. Two seven-foot bears singing bass is neither sight nor sound for the faint of heart. I noticed several people in the congregation perk up immediately.

With teeth and claws and fetid breath,
we now consign you unto death.

The children looked terrified, as well they might be. I think they might have been acting, but these guys looked pretty scary. However, it was at this point in the duet that Zeb's Bluetooth started to pick up police radio signals. I knew this because the two bears were scheduled to sing a repeat of their opening flourish, *Awake, awake!* What came out was:

Awake, awake! We have a ten fifty-seven on Elm.
Call for some back-up. Proceed with caution.

A moment later, Darius' Bluetooth picked up the same signal.

Roger that. Make ready then, thy bitter tomb,
And have thy prophet call for an ambulance.

I reached up, grabbed Dave's Blackberry off the harpsichord and tossed it into the baptismal font, a pretty good throw considering the font was a good five feet away. Now the bears couldn't hear, but at least they wouldn't be singing the police report.

"Braaaaap!" went the frog.

The children and the bears began the *Munching Dance*. The bears, having no idea there was a three-pound bullfrog under their feet, were happily stomping around in the way that bears do. Billy decided that, if one of the bears happened to get lucky, or *unlucky,* as the case may be, and end the frog's theatrical career, that would also be the end of the show. He slid down off the pew, all six foot-six, two-hundred sixty pounds of him, and crawled on his hands and knees toward the action.

Cynthia had taught the kids a very stately Baroque dance where each quartet held hands and stepped together in rhythm until one of the bears took a stylized swipe at one of them. Then that child would shriek, throw a red velvet streamer into the air to symbolize the slaughter of another youth-gone-wrong, and collapse in a heap. I knew the bears couldn't hear, but they were lumbering sorts, anyway, and not suited for dancing. Not like those Russian bears.

Moosey kept one eye on his pet and the other on the stomping paws of the bears. Billy, on the other hand, was intent on watching only the frog. If it jumped just a little farther his way...

"Braaaaap," went the frog, and took a mighty leap right toward Billy.

Moosey was in the group nearest the frog and jumped a split-second later. He might have caught Ribbet in mid-leap, had Billy not been attempting the same maneuver. The resulting crash took down the remaining dancers. They tossed their ribbons into the air with yelps of surprise. One of the bears, who was taking a slow swipe at Moosey, overbalanced when he wasn't there and tumbled to the floor in a sort of slow-motion somersault. The other bear, startled to be the only one standing, looked around in confusion, then reached down and helped his partner up. They stared at each other for a moment, then gave exagerated shrugs, and shuffled back down the aisle to join Elisha, who had retreated to the back of the sanctuary as per his stage instructions.

Moosey had a firm hold on the frog. Billy made it back to his pew, although we could still hear Elaine laughing from the balcony.

Right on cue, all of the children got up and stood in a straight line with Moosey in the middle. He turned Ribbet—miraculously unscathed—to face the audience, put his hands under the frog's arms, and held him up. The frog's long, amphibious fingers clung to Moosey the way a kitten might hang onto a branch after an ill-advised leap. Its white belly, mottled body and powerful legs dangled a good eighteen inches below Moosey's hands, and it looked out at the congregation with unblinking, bulbous eyes. Then Moosey lifted his pet aloft, took a deep breath, and sang to make angels weep.

Farewell mother, weep not for me,
For blessed Paradise I see.
To taunt Elish wrong were we,
And death our punishment must be.

The other children joined in:

With broken limbs and faces faire,
Now supper for the ancient bear,
We moan the curse that sealed our fate,
The mocking of his balding pate.

Mourn, all ye muses, make sad lament,
These youthful lives were foolish spent.
God's holy prophet man must never scorn,
Or else such Ursine fate must be by mankind borne.
Amen.

It was a service for the ages.

•••

"That was something," said Gaylen, when we'd all made it back to the parish hall for coffee, juice and general snacking. "I hope you're going to record it."

"I expect we will," I said. "It could have gone a little smoother."

"Nonsense," said Meg. "It went just as expected."

"Absolutely," agreed Bev.

"I need to go and talk to those Purcell Society members, I guess."

Meg gave me a puzzled look.

"They were sitting near the back on the right."

"Those were Garth and Garret's parents and two of their uncles. I talked to them after church."

"Hmm," I said. "I wonder what happened to the Purcell Society?"

"You mean Dr. Hiram Milligan?"

"Yeah." I paused. "Wait a minute. How did you know his name?"

Meg and Bev howled with laughter. "Don't you think Kent Murphee does a great Boston accent?"

"What?"

"I swear!" gasped Meg, between outbursts. "You are so gullible! The American Purcell Society? Oh, *really!*"

"Well," I grumbled. "It *could* have happened."

Chapter 22

"Thanks for surrendering," I said. "I'm glad you didn't make us come out and get you. The Boone P.D. will be here in a couple of minutes."

Nancy, Dave, Meg and I were sitting at our table in the Slab Café. Pete was behind the counter with Cynthia, listening in. Noylene was pouring us coffee.

"I'm sorry. Really, I am. He just made me so dang mad."

"He made everybody mad, Wormy," said Noylene sadly. "Twarn't no reason to kill him."

"Here's the thing, Noylene," Wormy said. "He was all the time hanging around our trailer. Then, with you getting pregnant and all..."

"What are you talking about?" said Noylene. "I hope you're not saying that this baby is Russ Stafford's."

"Well," said Wormy, angrily. "It sure as hell ain't mine! I figured it was Stafford's, for sure!"

"Sure it's yours, honey," said Noylene. "You went down and got re-tested, remember? Your little swimmers are A-okay."

"I went down and got re-tested all right. But I'm as sterile as a barrow in a nuclear corn crib."

"What?"

"I just *tol'* you I had my swimmers back," said Wormy. "So you'd co-sign that loan. But then I really *did* get tested." He shook his head sadly. "Nothin'."

Noylene lost a bit of her color, even though it had been recently applied at the Dip-n-Tan. She chewed on her bottom lip, but didn't say anything.

"So, if that baby ain't mine," said Wormy, "and it ain't Russ Stafford's, then whose is it?"

It was a question that begged answering, but the answer would have to wait. The cowbell jangled noisily against the glass door of the Slab, and Sgt. Todd McCay came in and walked over to the table.

"I sure am sorry about this, Wormy," he said.

Wormy stood up. "Yeah." He held out his wrists.

"No need for that," said Todd. "Hell, Judge Adams might even let you put up your Ferris wheel as a bond."

Wormy brightened as he followed Todd to the door. "You think so? That'd be great. I'll bet I can find those diamonds in another week or so. Then my troubles will be over!"

We watched silently as Todd put Wormy in the cruiser and pulled off into the twilight. Noylene stared for a minute, then took off her apron, tossed it on the counter, and walked out the front door.

"Okay, spill it," said Meg. "How did you know?"

"He as much as told us. I just wasn't paying attention."

Meg, Dave, Cynthia and Pete all looked at me like I had just been elected pope.

"Here's the thing," I said. "We were looking for someone who was at the Bible Bazaar. Someone who had motive and opportunity to kill Russ."

"Okay," said Nancy.

"We should have been looking for someone who *wasn't* at the Bible Bazaar."

"And who was that?" asked Dave.

"Skeeter Donalson."

"Why Skeeter?" asked Meg. "He was the leper."

"Sure he was," I said. "And the leper was working the crowd along with the beggar—Mitch St. Claire—just before the play started."

"So?" said Cynthia.

"So, it couldn't have been Skeeter because Skeeter was in the drunk tank in Boone. Wormy took him to a bar the night before and then got him arrested. Nancy didn't get him out till the next day."

"So it was the *leper*," said Meg. "With the rock, in the park. I thought it might be the butler."

"Skeeter had no motive," I said. "And there was no cause for us to even look at him. Wormy read the schedule, saw the title of the play and decided the time was right. It was easy to take Skeeter to a bar. Even easier to get him tossed in the drunk tank."

"Okay," said Nancy. "You knew it was someone dressed as the leper. What else?"

"I saw Wormy tossing a box full of rags into the dumpster beside the Beautifery. That's the second thing. He said they were left over from the Bible School. But he hadn't even been to the Bible Bazaar, and neither had Noylene, except to see that last play. Why would he have a box of rags?"

"The leper costume," said Cynthia, with a knowing look.

"That's also why there weren't any prints or DNA on the rock. Wormy covered his hands with those rags."

"Clever," said Dave.

"Also," I said, "you remember when Wormy said, 'that Russ Stafford's a snake or I ain't a capon?'"

"No," said Meg. Nancy and Dave shook their heads, as well.

"I remember," said Pete. "We were sitting right here."

"A capon. A castrated rooster. He knew he was sterile. He knew Noylene was pregnant, and he knew Russ Stafford was hanging around his house."

"Jealousy," said Dave. "Oldest story in the book."

"You sure are a smart'un, Sugar Cakes!" said Meg, giving me a kiss on the cheek.

"Sugar Cakes," snorted Nancy. "That's a new one!"

"How about some of that Boston cream pie?" I said. "On the house?"

"It's always on the house," grumbled Pete.

"That's why we love you, Pete," said Nancy.

Chapter 23

No one ever did find the diamond mine that Russ had stumbled upon—if, in fact, there ever was one—even though there were a lot of prospectors on Noylene's property throughout the entire summer. She collected a fat "prospecting fee" from each of them, had them sign an agreement giving her sixty percent of the proceeds of any gems found on her property, and still had plenty of business. Wormy DuPont pled guilty and ended up with a life sentence, so Noylene put Wormy Acres and the Ferris wheel up for sale. As to the father of her baby, that's another story.

Gerry Flemming took a plea agreement on the molestation charge and did a few months at a minimum security facility. By the time he got out, Wilma was long gone.

The Right Reverend Gaylen Weatherall came back to St. Germaine in July, as promised, and things returned to normal—or as normal as they ever were. She presided over four late summer weddings, a baptism, and a couple of funerals. Staff meetings were as efficient as they'd ever been under her righteous reign, although I tended to miss more than my share. I continued to choose the hymns, people continued to complain that they couldn't sing them, and all was right with the world.

The Bear and Brew reopened on a Sunday at the end of July with great fanfare and free beer. The referendum hadn't passed, but we had no law against *giving* away beer on a Sunday. No one picketed the event, and Brother Hog was even seen giving his special blessing to an Alaskan Pale Ale.

Bud McCollough went off to Davidson College in the fall. Pauli Girl readied herself for her senior year of high school, and Moosey decided that girls weren't so bad after all and spent the summer closely aligned with Bernadette.

As for Meg and me, we continued our journey toward our second anniversary. I pointed out that the traditional gift for the second anniversary was "cotton." She pointed out that whatever the traditional "cotton" was used as wrapping for had better be pretty impressive. I decided on emeralds. Diamonds? Nah. Only divas wore diamonds.

Postlude

"You sure you don't want that life insurance policy?" asked Marilyn. "If anything happens to you, I'll be out of a job. If you bought one, you could name me as beneficiary."

"If I did, how long do you think it would be before you accidentally shot me?" I asked.

"The policy says I have to wait six months," she said with a smile. "But it'll be the best six months of your life."

I lit a stogie and looked at Marilyn. Her hair resembled Granny Honeysuckle's famous tuna hot-dish: brown, dry and crisp around the edges, yellow and creamy in the center with just a hint of grease spilling out over the top. Her eyes were dancing like an old man shuffling for nickels outside a bus station bathroom. Her complexion was as perfect as newly mixed pancake batter spread smoothly across the griddle right before it bubbles up, except that it had a few lumps. Still, it was the best offer I'd had all day.

"Where do I sign?" I asked. It's good to be a detective.

About the Author

Mark Schweizer lives and works in Hopkinsville, Kentucky, where he composes, conducts a choir, writes the occasional book, and continues to be rabidly involved in church music.

He actually has a bunch of degrees, including a Doctor of Musical Arts from the University of Arizona. I *know!* What were they thinking?

The Liturgical Mysteries

The Alto Wore Tweed
Independent Mystery Booksellers Association "Killer Books" selection, 2004

The Baritone Wore Chiffon

The Tenor Wore Tapshoes
IMBA 2006 Dilys Award nominee

The Soprano Wore Falsettos
Southern Independent Booksellers Alliance 2007 Book Award Nominee

The Bass Wore Scales

The Mezzo Wore Mink

The Diva Wore Diamonds

Just A Note

If you've enjoyed this book—or any of the other mysteries in this series—please drop me a line. My e-mail address is mark@sjmp.com. Also, don't forget to visit the website (www.sjmpbooks.com) for lots of great stuff! You'll find recordings and "downloadable" music for many of the great works mentioned in the Liturgical Mysteries including *The Pirate Eucharist, The Weasel Cantata, The Mouldy Cheese Madrigal, The Banjo Kyrie* and a lot more.

Cheers,
Mark